"No other woman has ever made me feel the way you make me feel."

The words sent a thrill of satisfaction through her.

Alekos buried his face in her neck. "You were never this wild four years ago."

She was never this desperate. Kelly's eyes closed.

"Don't talk."

He welded his mouth to hers again, until she couldn't breathe or stand upright. Her hands closed over his shoulders, but what began as a need for support ended in a caress as her fingers slid over hard male muscle.

"Kelly—"

"Shut up."

She didn't want to talk about what they were doing. She wasn't sure she even wanted to think about it. Her teeth gritted as she ripped his shirt so that she could get to his chest, too absorbed by his body to bother undressing him.

To have sex with Alekos was to understand why her body had been invented.

His eyelids were lowered, eyes half shut as he watched her. It was a look of such raw sexual challenge that she shivered.

Later, she thought, I'm going to really regret this.

But right now she didn't care....

All about the author...
Sarah Morgan

SARAH MORGAN was born in Wiltshire and started writing at the age of eight when she produced an autobiography of her hamster.

At the age of eighteen she traveled to London to train as a nurse in one of London's top teaching hospitals, and she describes what happened in those years as extremely happy and definitely censored!

She worked in a number of areas after she qualified, but her favorite was A&E where she found the work stimulating and fun. Nowhere else in the hospital environment did she encounter such good teamwork between doctors and nurses.

By now her interests had moved on from hamsters to men, and she started writing romance fiction.

Her first completed manuscript, written after the birth of her first child, was rejected by Harlequin® Books but the comments were encouraging, so she tried again, and on the third attempt her manuscript *Worth the Risk* was accepted unchanged. She describes receiving the acceptance letter as one of the best moments of her life, after meeting her husband and having her two children.

Sarah still works part-time in a health-related industry and spends the rest of the time with her family trying to squeeze in writing whenever she can. She is an enthusiastic skier and walker and loves outdoor life.

Sarah Morgan

ONE NIGHT...
NINE-MONTH SCANDAL

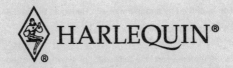

HARLEQUIN®

TORONTO • NEW YORK • LONDON
AMSTERDAM • PARIS • SYDNEY • HAMBURG
STOCKHOLM • ATHENS • TOKYO • MILAN • MADRID
PRAGUE • WARSAW • BUDAPEST • AUCKLAND

Recycling programs
for this product may
not exist in your area.

ISBN-13: 978-0-373-12943-0

ONE NIGHT...NINE-MONTH SCANDAL

First North American Publication 2010.

This edition published by arrangement with Harlequin Books S.A.

For questions and comments about the quality of this book please contact us at Customer_eCare@Harlequin.ca.

www.eHarlequin.com

Printed in U.S.A.

ONE NIGHT...
NINE-MONTH SCANDAL

CHAPTER ONE

'I DON'T care if he's on a conference call, this is urgent!'

The voice outside his office belonged to his lawyer and Alekos paused in mid-sentence as the door burst open.

Dmitri stood there, papers in his hand, his face a strange shade of scarlet.

'I'll call you back,' Alekos drawled and hit the button to disconnect himself from his team in New York and London. 'Given that I've never seen you run anywhere in the ten years you've worked for me, I assume you're the bearer of bad tidings. A tanker has sunk?'

'Quickly.' The normally calm, steady Dmitri sprinted across the spacious office, banged into the desk and spilled the papers over the floor. 'Switch on your computer.'

'I'm already online.' Intrigued, Alekos shifted his gaze to his computer screen. 'What am I supposed to be looking at?'

'Go to eBay,' Dmitri said in a strangled voice. 'Right now. We have three minutes left to bid.'

Alekos didn't waste time pointing out that placing bids with an online auction-house didn't usually form part of his working day. Instead he accessed the site with a few taps of his fingers.

'Diamond,' Dmitri croaked. 'Type in "large, white diamond".'

A premonition forming in his mind, Alekos stabbed the keys. No; she couldn't have. *She wouldn't have.*

As the page sprang onto his screen, he swore softly in Greek while Dmitri sank uninvited onto the nearest chair. 'Am I right? Is it the Zagorakis diamond? Being sold on eBay?'

Alekos stared at the stone and felt emotion punch deep in his gut. Just seeing that ring made him think of *her*, and thinking of her set off a chain reaction in his body that shocked him with its intensity. He struggled to shake off the instantaneous assault on his senses triggered by those rebel thoughts. Even after four years of absence she could still do this to him, he thought grimly. 'It's the diamond. You're sure she is the seller?'

'It would appear so. If the stone had come on the market before now we would have been notified. I have a team checking it out right now, but the bids have already reached a million dollars. Why eBay?' Bending down, Dmitri gathered together the papers he'd dropped. 'Why not Christie's or Sotheby's, or one of the big, reputable auction-houses? It's a very strange decision.'

'Not strange.' His eyes fixed on the screen, Alekos laughed. 'It's entirely in character. She'd never go to Christie's or Sotheby's.' Her down to earth approach had been one of the things he'd found so refreshing about her. She'd been unpretentious—an attribute that was a rare commodity in the false, glittering world he inhabited.

'Well, whichever.' Dmitri tugged at his tie as if he were being strangled. 'If bids have reached a million dollars then there's a high probability that someone else knows this is the Zagorakis diamond. We have to stop her! Why is she doing this now? Why not four years ago? She had plenty of reason to hate you then.'

Alekos leaned back in his chair, considering that question. When he spoke, his voice was soft. 'She saw the pictures.'

'Of you and Marianna at the charity ball? You think she heard the rumours that the relationship is serious?'

Alekos stared at the ring taunting him from the screen. 'Yes.'

The ring said it all. Its presence on the screen said *this is what I think of what we shared.* It was the equivalent of flinging the diamond into the river, only far, far more effective. She was selling it to the highest bidder in the most public way possible and her message was clear: this ring means nothing to me.

Our relationship meant nothing.

She was in a wild fury.

His own anger slashed like the blade of a knife and he stood up suddenly, taking this latest gesture as confirmation that he'd made the right choice with Marianna. Marianna Konstantin would never do anything as vulgar as sell a ring on eBay. Marianna was far too discreet and well-bred to give away a gift. Her behaviour was always impeccable; she was quiet and restrained, miserly with her emotions and, most importantly, she didn't want to get married.

Alekos stared at the ring on the screen, guessing at the depth of emotion hidden behind the sale. Nothing restrained there. The woman selling his ring gave her emotions freely.

Remembering just how freely, his mouth tightened. It would be good, he thought, to cut that final link. This was the time.

Watching the clock count down on his computer screen, Alekos made an instantaneous decision. 'Bid for it, Dmitri.'

His lawyer floundered. 'Bid? How? You need an account, and there is no time to set one up.'

'We need someone just out of college.' Swift and decisive, Alekos pressed a button on his phone. 'Send Eleni in. Now.'

Seconds later, the youngest PA on his team appeared nervously in the doorway. 'You wanted to speak to me, Mr Zagorakis?'

'Do you have an eBay account?'

Clearly stunned by the unexpected question, the girl gulped. 'Yes, sir.'

'I need you to bid for something. And don't call me sir.' His eyes on the screen, Alekos watched as the clock ticked down: two minutes. He had two minutes in which to retrieve something that should never have left his possession. 'Log in, or whatever it is you do to put in a bid.'

'Yes, sir. Of course.' Crumbling with nerves, the girl hurried to his desk and entered her username and password. She was shaking so badly that she entered her password incorrectly and Alekos clamped his mouth shut, sensing that if he showed impatience he'd just make her more nervous.

'Take your time,' he said smoothly, sending a warning glance towards Dmitri who looked as if he were about to have a stroke.

Finally entering her password correctly, the girl gave him a terrified smile. 'What bid do you want me to place?'

Alekos looked at the screen and made a judgement. 'Two-million US dollars.'

The girl gave an audible gasp. *'How much?'*

'Two million.' Alekos watched the clock counting down: sixty seconds. He had sixty seconds to retrieve an heirloom that he never should have given away. Sixty seconds to close the door on a relationship that never should have happened. 'Do it now.'

'But the limit on my credit card is only f-five hundred pounds,' the girl stammered, 'I can't afford it.'

'But I can. And I'm the one paying for it.' Glancing at the girl's ashen features, Alekos frowned. 'Do *not* pass out. If you faint now, I won't be able to bid for this ring. Dmitri is head of my legal team—he will witness my verbal agreement. We now have thirty seconds, and this is very important to me. Please.'

'Of course, I—sorry.' Her hands shaking, Eleni tapped the amount into the box, hesitated briefly and then pressed enter. 'I—I'm—I mean *you're*—currently the highest bidder,' she said faintly and Alekos lifted an eyebrow.

'Is it done?'

'Providing no one puts in a last-minute bid.'

Alekos, who wasn't taking any chances, promptly put his hands over hers and entered four-million dollars.

Five seconds later, the ring was his and he was pouring the shaking girl a glass of water.

'I'm impressed. Under pressure you responded well and you did what needed to be done. I won't forget it.

And now,' he kept his voice casual, 'I need to know exactly where to send the money. Does the seller give you a name and address?'

Ignoring Dmitri's startled glance, Alekos reached for a pen and paper.

He needed to decide whether to do this in person or hand it over to lawyers.

Lawyers, his common sense told him. *For all the reasons you haven't tracked her whereabouts over the past four years.*

'You can email any questions you have,' Eleni said weakly, her eyes on the diamond on the screen. 'It's a beautiful ring. Lucky woman, ending up with that on her finger. Wow. That's so romantic.' She looked at him wide-eyed and Alekos didn't have the heart to disillusion her.

Had he ever been romantic? If being romantic was to indulge in an impulsive, whirlwind romance then, yes, he'd been romantic. Once. Or maybe 'blinded by lust' would be a more accurate assessment. Fortunately he'd come to his senses in time. With a cynical smile at his own expense, Alekos reflected on the fact that a business approach to relationships, such as the one he had with Marianna, was vastly preferable. He'd had no particular wish to understand her, and she'd showed no interest in trying to understand him.

That was so much better than a girl who tried to climb into your thoughts and then seduced with raw, out-of-control sex that wiped a man's brain.

Feeling the tension ripple across his shoulders, Alekos stared out of the window as Dmitri hastily ushered the girl out of the room, promising to deal with all the financial aspects of the transaction.

Closing the door firmly, the lawyer turned to face Alekos. 'I'll arrange for the funds to be transferred and the ring collected.'

'No.' Driven by an impulse he decided was better not examined, Alekos reached for his jacket. 'I don't want that ring in the hands of a third party. I'll collect it myself.'

'In person? Alekos, you haven't seen the girl for four years. You decided it was best not to get in touch. Are you sure this is a good idea?'

'I only ever have good ideas.' Closure, Alekos thought grimly, striding towards the door. Hand over the money, take the ring and move on.

'Breathe, breathe, breathe. Put your head between your legs—that's it. You're *not* going to faint. OK—that's good. Now, try telling me again—slowly.'

Lifting her head, Kelly mouthed the words. No sound came out. She wondered whether it was possible to go mute with shock. It felt as though her entire body had shut down.

Her friend glared at her in exasperation. 'Kel, I'm giving you thirty seconds to produce sound from your mouth and then I'm throwing a bucket of water over you.'

Kelly dragged in air and tried again. 'Sold—'

Vivien nodded encouragingly. 'You've sold some-thing—right. What have you sold?'

'Sold.' Kelly swallowed. 'Ring.'

'OK, *finally* we're making progress here—I'm getting that you've sold a ring. Which ring?' Viv's eyes suddenly widened. 'Holy crap, not *the* ring?'

Kelly nodded, feeling as though all the air had been sucked out of the room. 'Sold ring—eBay.' She felt dizzy and light-headed, and she knew she would have been lying on the floor in a dead faint by now if she hadn't already been sitting down.

'All right, well, that's good.' Her expression cautious, Vivien's smile faltered. 'I can understand why that seems like such a big thing. You've been wearing that ring around your neck for four years—which is probably four years too long given that the rat who gave it to you didn't turn up for the wedding—but you've finally seen the light and sold it, and I think that's great. Nothing to worry about. No reason to hyperventilate. Do you need to breathe into a paper bag or something?' She looked at Kelly dubiously. 'You're the same colour as a whiteboard, and I'm rubbish at first aid. I closed my eyes in all the classes because I couldn't stand the revolting pictures. Am I supposed to slap you? Or do I stick your legs in the air to help blood flow? Give me some clues here. I know the whole thing traumatised you, but it's been four years, for crying out loud!'

Kelly gulped and clutched her friend's hand. 'Sold.'

'Yes, yes, I know! *You sold the ring!* Just get over it! Now you can get on with your life—go out and shag some stranger to celebrate. It's time you realised that Mr Greek God isn't the only man in the world.'

'For four-million dollars.'

'Or we could just open a bottle of—*what? How much?*' Vivien's voice turned to a squeak and she plopped onto the floor, her mouth open. 'For a moment there I thought you actually said four-million dollars.'

'I did. Four-million dollars.' Saying the words aloud doubled the shaking. 'Vivien, I don't feel very well.'

'I don't feel very well either.' Vivien gave a whimper and flapped her hand in front of her face. 'We can't both faint. We might bang our heads or something, and our decomposed bodies would be discovered weeks from now, and no one would even find us because your place is always such a mess. I bet you haven't even made a will. I mean, all I own is a load of unwashed laundry and a few bills, but *you* have four-million dollars. Four-million dollars. God, I've never had a rich friend before. Now I'm the one who needs to breathe.' She grabbed a paper bag, emptied out two apples and slammed it over her mouth and nose, breathing in and out noisily.

Kelly stared down at her hands, wondering if they'd stop shaking if she sat on them. They'd been shaking since she'd switched on her computer and seen the final bid. 'I—I need to pull myself together. I can't just sit here shaking. I have work to do. I have thirty English books to mark before tomorrow.'

Vivien pulled the bag away from her face and sucked in air. 'Don't be ridiculous. You never have to teach small children again. You can be a lady of leisure. You can walk in there tomorrow, resign and go for a spa day. Or a spa decade!'

'I wouldn't do that.' Shocked, Kelly stared at her friend, the full implications of the money sinking home. 'I love teaching. I'm the only one not looking forward to the summer holidays. I *love* the kids. I'll miss the kids. They're the nearest I'm ever going to get to a family of my own.'

'For crying out loud, Kel, you're twenty-three, not ninety. And, anyway, you're rich now. You'll be a toy girl, or a sugar mummy or something. Men will be queuing up to impregnate you.'

Kelly recoiled. 'You don't have a romantic bone in your body, do you?'

'I'm a realist. And I know you love kids. Weird, really; I just want to bash their heads together most of the time. Maybe you should just give me the money and *I'll* resign. Four million dollars! How come you didn't know it was worth that much?'

'I didn't ask,' Kelly mumbled. 'The ring was special because he gave it to me, not because of its value. It didn't occur to me it was that valuable. I wasn't really interested.'

'You need to learn to be practical as well as romantic. He might have been a bastard, but at least he wasn't a cheapskate.' Vivien sank her teeth into one of the apples that she'd tipped out of the paper bag, talking as she ate. 'When you told me he was Greek, I assumed he was a waiter or something.'

Kelly flushed. She hated talking about it because it reminded her of how stupid she'd been. How *naive*. 'He wasn't a waiter.' She covered her face with her hands. 'I can't even bear to think about it. How could I ever have thought it could have worked? He is super-cool, super-intelligent and super-rich. I'm not super-anything.'

'Yes you are,' Vivien said loyally. 'You're—you're, um, super-messy, super-scatterbrained and—'

'Shut up! I don't need to hear any more reasons why it didn't work.' Kelly wondered how anything could possibly still hurt this much after four years. 'It would be nice if I could think of just one reason why it might have worked.'

Vivien took a large bit of apple and chewed thoughtfully. 'You have super-big breasts?'

Kelly covered her chest with her arms. 'Thanks,' she muttered, not knowing whether to laugh or cry.

'You're welcome. So how did Mr Super Rich make his money?'

'Shipping. He owns a shipping company—a big one. Lots of ships.'

'Don't tell me—super-big ones? Why did you never tell me this before?' Munching away, Vivien shook her head in disbelief. 'This guy was multi-millionaire, wasn't he?'

Kelly rubbed her foot on the threadbare carpet of her tiny flat. 'I read somewhere he was a billionaire.'

'Oh, right—well, who's counting? What's a few-hundred million between friends? So—don't take this the wrong way—how did *you* meet him? I've been alive the same number of years as you and I've never met a single millionaire, let alone a billionaire. Some tips would be welcome.'

'It was during my gap year. I trespassed on his private beach. I didn't know it was private; I'd left my guide book somewhere and I was in a bit of a dream, looking at the view, not reading the signs.' Misery oozed through her veins. 'Can we talk about something else? It isn't my favourite subject.'

'Sure. We can talk about what you're going to do with four-million dollars.'

'I don't know.' Kelly gave a helpless shrug. 'Pay for a psychiatrist to treat me for shock?'

'Who bought the thing?'

Kelly looked at her blankly, worried that her brain appeared to have stalled. 'Someone rich?'

Viven looked at her with exasperation. 'And when do you hand it over?'

'Some girl emailed me to say it would be collected in person tomorrow. I gave them the address of the school in case they turn out to be dodgy.' She pressed her hand to the ring that she wore on a chain under her shirt and Vivien sighed.

'You never take it off. You even sleep in the thing.'

'That's because I have a problem with my personal organisation,' Kelly said in a small voice. 'I'm afraid I might lose it.'

'If you're trying to hide behind the "I'm untidy" act, forget it. I know you're untidy, but you wear the ring because you're still stuck on him, and you've been stuck on him for four years. What made you suddenly decide to sell the ring, Kel? What happened? You've been acting awfully weird all week.'

Kelly swallowed hard and fiddled with the ring through her shirt. 'I saw pictures of him with another woman,' she said thickly. 'Blonde, stick-thin—you know the type. The sort that makes you want to stop eating, until you realise that even if you stopped eating you still wouldn't look like that.' She sniffed, 'I suddenly realised that keeping the ring was stopping me from moving on with my life. It's crazy. *I'm* crazy.'

'No, not any more. Finally you're sane.' Vivien sprang to her feet and flung her hair out of her eyes in a dramatic gesture. 'You know what this means, don't you?'

'I need to pull myself together and forget about him?'

'It means no more cheap pasta with sauce from a jar. Tonight we're eating takeaway pizza with extra toppings, and you're paying. Yay!' Vivien reached for the phone. 'Bring on the high life.'

Alekos Zagorakis stepped out of his black Ferrari and stared at the old Victorian building.

Hampton Park First School.

Of course she would have chosen to work with children. What else?

It had been the day he'd read in the press that she was planning on four children that he'd walked out on her.

With a grim smile that was entirely at his own expense, he scanned the building, automatically noticing the things that needed doing. The fence was torn in several places and plastic covered one section of the roof, presumably to prevent a leak. But the surroundings weren't responsible for the ripple of tension that spread across his shoulders.

A bell rang, and less than a minute later a stream of children poured through the swing doors and into the playground, jostling and elbowing each other. A young woman followed the children out of the door, answering questions, refereeing arguments and gently admonishing when things grew out of hand. She was dressed in a simple black skirt, flat shoes and a nondescript shirt. Alekos didn't give her a second glance. He was too busy looking for Kelly.

He studied the ancient buildings, deciding that his information must be wrong. Why would Kelly bury herself in a place like this?

He was about to return to his car when he heard a familiar laugh. His eyes followed the sound, and suddenly he found himself taking a closer look at the young teacher in the black skirt and sensible heels.

She bore no resemblance to the carefree teenager he'd met on the beach in Corfu, and he was about to dismiss her again when she tilted her head.

Alekos stared at her hair, fiercely repressed by a clip at the back of her head. If that clip was released and her hair fell forward... He frowned, mentally stripping off the drab garments so that he could see the woman concealed beneath.

Then she smiled, and he sucked in a sharp breath because it was impossible not to recognise that smile. It was wide, warm and generous, freely bestowed and genuine. Dragging his eyes from her mouth, Alekos took a second look at the sensible skirt. He could see now that she had the same long, long legs. Legs designed to make a man lose the thread of his conversation and his focus. *Legs that had once been wrapped around his waist.*

Shouts of excitement snapped him out of his perusal of her wardrobe. A group of boys had noticed the car, and instantly he regretted not having parked it round the corner out of sight. As they sprinted across the playground to the flimsy fence that separated the school from the outside world, Alekos stared at them as another man might stare at a dangerous animal.

Three little heads stared at him and then the car.

'Wow—cool car.'

'Is it a Porsche? My dad says the best car is a Porsche.'

'When I grow up, I'm going to have one like this.'

Alekos had no idea what to say to them so he stood still, frozen by his own inadequacy as they rattled the fence, small fingers curling between the wire as they stared and admired.

He saw her head turn as she checked anxiously on her charges. Of course, she would notice instantly when one of her flock had wandered from safety. She was that sort of person. A people person. She was messy, scatty, noisy and caring. And she wouldn't have greeted a group of children with silence.

She saw the car first and Alekos watched as the colour fled her face, the sudden pallor of her skin accentuating the unusual sapphire-blue of her eyes.

Obviously she didn't know any other men who drove a Ferrari, he thought grimly. The fact that she was shocked to see him increased his anger.

What had she expected, that he'd sit by and watch the ring—*the ring he'd put on her finger*—sold to the highest bidder?

Across that stretch of nondescript tarmac, that school playground that was no one's idea of a romantic venue for a reunion, wide blue eyes met fierce black.

The sun came out from beyond a cloud, sending a spotlight of bright gold onto her shining head. It reminded him of the way she'd looked that afternoon on his beach in Corfu. She'd been wearing a miniscule, turquoise bikini and a pretty, unselfconscious smile.

With no desire to climb aboard that train of thought, Alekos dragged his mind back to the present.

'Boys!' Her voice was melting chocolate with hints of cinnamon—smooth with a hint of spice. 'Don't climb the fence! You know it's dangerous.'

Alekos felt the thud of raw emotion in his gut. Four years ago she would have hurled herself across the playground with the enthusiasm of a puppy and thrown herself into his arms.

The fact that she was now looking at him as if he'd escaped from a tiger reserve added an extra boost to his rocketing tension-levels.

Alekos looked at the boy nearest to him, the need for information unlocking his tongue. 'Is she your teacher?'

'Yes, she's our teacher.' Despite the warning, the boy jammed the toe of his shoe in the wire fence and tried to climb up. 'She doesn't look strict, but if you do something wrong—pow!' He slammed his fist into his palm and Alekos felt a stab of shock.

'She hits you?'

'Are you kidding?' The boy collapsed with laughter at the thought. 'She won't even squash a spider. She catches them in a glass and lifts them out of the classroom. She never even shouts.'

'You said "pow".'

'Miss Jenkins has a way of squashing you with a look. Pow!' The boy shrugged. 'She makes you feel bad if you've done something wrong. Like you've let her down. But she'd never hurt anyone. She's non-violent.'

Non-violent. Miss Jenkins.

Alekos inhaled sharply; so, she wasn't married. She didn't yet have the four children she wanted.

Only now that the question was answered did he acknowledge that the possibility had been playing on his mind.

She crossed the playground towards him as if she were being dragged by an invisible rope. It was obvious that, given the chance, she would have run in the opposite direction. 'Freddie, Kyle, Colin.' She addressed the three boys in a firm tone that left no doubt about her abilities to manage a group of high-spirited children, 'Come away from the fence.'

There was a clamour of conversation and he noticed that she answered their questions, instead of hushing them impatiently as so many adults did. And the children clearly adored her.

'Have you seen the car, Miss Jenkins? It's soo cool. I've only ever seen one in a picture.'

'It's just a car. Four wheels and an engine. Colin, I'm not telling you again.' Turning her head, she looked at Alekos, her smile completely false. 'How can I help you?'

She'd always been hopeless at hiding her feelings, and he read her as easily now as he had four years ago.

She was horrified to see him, and Alekos felt his temper burn like a jet engine.

'Feeling guilty, *agape mou*?'

'Guilty?'

'You don't seem pleased to see me,' he said silkily. 'I wonder why.'

Two bright spots of colour appeared on her cheeks and her eyes were suddenly suspiciously bright. 'I have nothing to say to you.'

He should have greeted that ingenuous remark with the appropriate degree of contempt, but the ring had somehow faded in his mind, and now he was thinking something else entirely. Something hot, dangerous and primitive that only ever came into his head when he was with her.

Their eyes locked and he knew she was thinking the same thing. The moment held them both captive, and then she looked away, her cheeks as fiercely pink as they had been white a few moments earlier. She was treating him as if she didn't know why he was here. As if they hadn't once been intimately acquainted. *As if there wasn't a single part of her body that he didn't know.*

A tiny voice piped up. 'Is he your boyfriend, miss?'

'Freddie Harrison, that is an extremely personal question!' Flustered, she urged the children away from the fence with a movement of her hand. 'This is Alekos Zagorakis, and he is *not* my boyfriend. He is just someone I knew a long time ago.'

'A friend, miss?'

'Um, yes, a *friend*.' The word was dragged from her and the children looked suddenly excited.

'Miss Jenkins has a boyfriend, Miss Jenkins has a boyfriend...' the chant increased the tension in her eyes.

'Friend is not the same as boyfriend, Freddie.'

'Of course it's not the same thing.' One of the boys snorted. 'If it's a boyfriend, you have sex, stupid.'

'Miss, he said the sex word *and* he called me stupid. You said no one was to call anyone stupid!'

She dealt with the quarrel skilfully and dispatched the children to play before turning back to Alekos. Glancing quickly over her shoulder to check that she couldn't be overheard, she stepped closer to the fence. 'I cannot *believe* you had the nerve to come here after four years.' Every part of her was shaking, her hands, her knees, her voice. 'How could you be so horribly, hideously insensitive? If it weren't for the fact the children are watching, I'd punch you—which is probably why you came here instead of somewhere private. You're scared I'd hurt you. What are you *doing* here?'

'You know why I'm here. And you've never punched anyone in your life, Kelly.' It was one of the things that had drawn him to her. Her gentleness had been an antidote to the ruthless, cut-throat business-world he inhabited.

'There's always a first time, and this might well be it.' She lifted her hand to her chest and pressed it there, as if she were checking that her heart was still beating. 'Just get it over with, will you? Say what you have to say and go.'

Distracted by the press of her breasts against her plain white shirt, Alekos frowned. It was virtually buttoned to the throat; it was perfectly decent. There was nothing, absolutely nothing, about what she was wearing that could explain the volcanic response of his libido.

Infuriated with both himself and her, his tone was sharper than usual. 'Don't play games with me, because we both know who will win. I'll eat you for breakfast.'

It was the wrong analogy. The moment the words left his mouth, he had an uncomfortably clear memory of her lying naked on his bed, the remains of breakfast scattered over the sheets as he took his pleasure in an entirely different way.

The hot colour in her cheeks told him that she was remembering exactly the same incident.

'You don't eat breakfast,' she said hoarsely. 'You just drink that vile, thick Greek coffee. And I don't want to play anything with you. You don't play by the same rules as anyone else. You—you're a *snake*!'

Struggling with his physical reaction to her, Alekos stared down into her wide eyes and realised in a blinding flash that she genuinely didn't know he was the one who had bought the ring.

With a cynical laugh at his own expense, he dragged his hand through his hair and swore softly to himself in Greek.

That was what happened, he reminded himself grimly, when he forgot that Kelly didn't think like other people. His skill at thinking ahead, at second guessing people, was one of the reasons for his phenomenal business success, but with Kelly it was a skill that had failed him. She didn't think the way other women thought. She'd surprised him, over and over again. And she was surprising him now. Seeing the sheen of tears in her eyes, he sucked in a breath, realising with a blinding flash of intuition that she hadn't sold the ring to send him a message. She'd sold the ring because he'd hurt her.

In that single moment, Alekos knew that he'd made a grave error of judgement. He should not have come here in person. It wasn't easy on him, and it wasn't fair on her. 'You have four-million dollars of my money in your bank account,' he said calmly, resolving to get this finished as quickly as possible for both their sakes. He watched as shock turned her eyes a darker shade of blue. 'I've come for my ring.'

CHAPTER TWO

KELLY stood in the classroom, gulping in air.

Alekos had bought the ring?

No, no, *no*! That wasn't possible. Was it? Thumping her fist to her forehead, she tried to think straight, wondering why it hadn't occurred to her that it could be him.

Because billionaires didn't trawl eBay, that was why. If she'd thought for a moment that he would find out about it, she would never have sold it.

As the full consequences of her actions hit her, Kelly gave a low moan.

Instead of purging him from her life, she'd brought him back into it.

When she'd seen him standing at the fence, she'd almost passed out. For one crazy moment she'd thought he was there to tell her he'd changed his mind. That he'd made a mistake. *That he was sorry.*

Sorry.

Kelly covered her hand with her mouth and stifled a hysterical laugh. When had Alekos ever said sorry? Had he even mentioned the tiny fact that he hadn't turned up at the wedding? No. There hadn't been a hint of apology in his indecently handsome face.

'Are you all right, miss?' A small voice cut through her panic. 'You look sort of weird and you ran in here like someone was after you.'

'After me?' Kelly licked dry lips. 'No.'

'You look like you're hiding.'

'I'm not hiding.' Her voice was high-pitched and she stared at her class without seeing them. Why, oh why, had she run away? Now it was going to look as though she really cared, and she didn't want him thinking that. She wanted him to think that she was doing fine and that breaking up with him had done nothing but improve her life. That selling her ring had been part of de-cluttering, or something.

Kelly tried to breathe steadily. She'd spent four years dreaming about seeing him again. She'd lain in bed at night imagining bumping into him—a feat which had really challenged the imagination, given that he moved in a different stratosphere. But never, not once, had she actually thought it might happen. Certainly not here, without warning.

'Is there a fire, Miss Jenkins?' A pair of worried eyes stared at her—little Jessie Prince who always worried about everything, from spelling tests to terrorists. 'You were running. You always tell us we're not supposed to run unless there's a fire, Miss Jenkins.'

'That's right.' Fire, and men you never wanted to see again. 'And I wasn't running, I was, er, walking very quickly. Power walking. It's good for fitness.' Was he still outside the school? *What if he waited for her?* 'Open your English books. Turn to page twelve and we'll carry on where we left off. We're writing our own poem about the summer holidays.' Maybe she should have just handed him the ring, but that would have meant revealing the fact she was wearing it round her neck, and there was no way she was giving him the satisfaction of knowing what it meant to her. The only thing she had left was her pride.

There was a rustle of paper, a hum of low chatter and then a loud commotion at the back of the class.

'Ow! He punched me, miss!'

Kelly lifted her hand to her forehead and breathed deeply. *Not now.* Discipline problems were the last thing she needed. Her head throbbed and she felt sick. She desperately needed space to think, but if there was one thing teaching didn't give you it was space. 'Tom, come to the front of the class, please.' She waited patiently while he dragged his feet towards her sulkily, and then crouched down in front of the little boy. 'You don't just go around punching people. It's wrong. I want you to say sorry.'

'But I'm *not* sorry.' He glared at her mutinously, his scarlet cheeks clashing with his vivid hair. 'He called me a carrot-head, Miss Jenkins.'

Finding it almost impossible to focus, Kelly took a deep breath. 'That wasn't nice, and he's going to apologise too. But that doesn't change the fact you punched him. You should never punch anyone.'

Not even arrogant Greek men who left you on your wedding day.

'S'not my fault I've got a temper. It's cos of my red hair.'

'It's not your hair that punched Harry.' *How had she been supposed to know he was the one who had bought the ring?*

A child behind her piped up. 'My dad says if someone is mean to you, you should just thump them and then they'll never been mean to you again.'

Kelly sighed. 'Alternatively we could all just try and think more about each other's feelings.' Raising her voice slightly, she addressed the whole class. 'We need to understand that not everyone is the same. We need to show tolerance: that's going to be our word for the day.' She stood and walked to the front of the class, feeling twenty-six pairs of eyes boring into her back. 'T-o-l-e-r-a-n-c-e. Who can tell me what it means?'

Twenty-six hands shot up.

'Miss, miss, I know—pick me, pick me.'

Kelly hid a smile. It didn't matter how stressed she was, they always made her smile. 'Jason?'

'Miss, that man is at the door.'

Twenty-six little necks craned to get a better view of their visitor.

Kelly glanced up just as Alekos yanked open the door and strode into the room.

Mute with horror, she just stared at him, registering with numb despair the sudden increase in her pulse rate. *Was this how her mother had felt about her father?* Had she felt this same rush of excitement even though she knew the relationship was hopeless?

Alekos changed the atmosphere in a room, Kelly thought dizzily. His presence commanded attention.

There was a discordant scraping of chairs and desks as the children all stood up and Kelly felt a lump in her throat as she saw them looking at her for approval. When she'd first taken over the class, they'd been a disjointed rabble. Now they were a team.

'Well done, class,' she said huskily. 'Lovely manners. Everyone gets two stars in their book.' It comforted her, having them there. It gave her strength to turn and face Alekos as he strode towards her. 'This isn't a good time. I'm teaching.'

'It's a perfectly good time for me.' His eyes clashed with hers; Kelly felt her face turn scarlet and her legs tremble violently as she remembered the passion they'd shared.

She held onto her composure for the benefit of the twenty-six pairs of watching eyes. 'We have a visitor—what didn't he do?'

'He didn't knock, Miss Jenkins.'

'That's right.' Kelly conjured a bright smile, like a magician pulling a rabbit from a hat. 'He didn't knock. He forgot his manners and he broke the rules. So he and I are just going to pop outside so that I can give him a little lesson on the behaviour we expect in our classroom, and you're going to finish writing your poem.'

She turned to leave the room but Alekos closed his hand around her wrist, dragging her against his side as he faced the goggle-eyed children.

'Let me teach you all a really important life lesson, children.' His Greek accent was more pronounced than usual, his eyes dark, as he surveyed the class with the same concentration and focus that he undoubtedly brought to his own boardroom. 'When something is important to you, you go for it. You don't let someone walk away from you, and you don't stand outside a door waiting for permission to enter. You just do it.'

This unusually radical approach was greeted with stunned, fascinated silence. Then several little arms shot into the air.

Alekos blinked. 'Yes, you?' Rising to the challenge, he pointed to a boy in the front row.

'But what if there are *rules*?'

'If they're not sensible, then you break them,' Alekos said immediately and Kelly gasped.

'No! You do not break them. Rules are there to—'

'Be questioned,' Alekos said with arrogant assurance, his deep male voice holding the children transfixed. '*Always* you must question and ask yourself "why?" Sometimes rules must be broken for progress to be made. Sometimes people will tell you that you can't do something. Are you going to listen?'

Twenty-six heads moved from side to side doubtfully and Kelly tugged at her wrist, trying to disengage herself so that she could take control.

A choked laugh bubbled up in her throat. Who was she kidding? She was never going to be able to gain control in the classroom again.

Alekos didn't release her. 'Take now, for example. I need to talk to Miss Jenkins, and she doesn't want to listen. What am I going to do? Am I going to walk away?'

A hand shot up. 'It depends how important it is to speak to her.'

'It is very important.' Alekos emphasised each word carefully as he addressed the captivated class. 'But it's also important to make the other person feel they are having a say in what happens, so I am willing to concede a point. I will let her choose where we have the conversation. Kelly?' He turned to face her, his eyes glittering dark. 'Here or outside?'

'Outside.' Kelly spoke through clenched teeth and Alekos smiled and turned back to the children.

'This is an example of a successful negotiation: it should be a win-win situation. We both have something we want. And now I am going to take Miss Jenkins outside and you are going to—to write one-hundred words on why rules should *always* be questioned.'

'No, they're not!' Kelly made a choked sound in her throat. 'They're going to write their poem.'

'Fine.' His eyes lingered on her mouth for a moment before sliding back to the enraptured class. 'You can write a poem—about the benefit of breaking rules. It was very nice to meet you all. Work hard and you will succeed in life. Remember—it's not where you come from that matters, it's where you're going.' His hand still locked around Kelly's wrist, he strode back out of the classroom giving her no choice but to follow him.

Outside the classroom, she leaned against the wall, shaking. 'I can't *believe* you just did that.'

'You're welcome,' he drawled. 'My going rate for motivational speaking on the international circuit is half a million dollars, but in this case I'm willing to waive my fee for the benefit of the next generation.'

Kelly's mouth opened and shut. 'I wasn't thanking you!'

'Well, you should be. Tomorrow's entrepreneurs won't emerge from a group of rule enslaved robots.' Studying her face, he gave a sardonic smile. 'Something tells me I'm not going to be given two stars in my book.'

Almost exploding with frustration, Kelly curled her hands into fists. 'Don't you know *anything* about children?'

The smile disappeared along with the mockery. Without it his face was cold, hard and handsome. 'No.' His voice was taut and his expression suddenly guarded. 'Nothing. I spoke to them as adults, not children.'

'But they're not adults, Alekos. Do you know how much trouble we have with discipline?' She was desperately aware of his fingers on her wrist and the sexy look in his eyes as he looked down at her. 'When I took over that class they couldn't even sit still on a chair for five minutes.'

'Sitting still is an overrated pastime. Even in board meetings I often walk around. It helps me think. You should be encouraging them to question, not trying to churn out obedient clones all doing as they're told. *Why* did you sell my ring?'

Kelly studiously ignored his question. 'Without rules, society would fall apart.'

'And without people bold enough to break rules, society would never progress,' he purred. 'And I'm not here to—' Before he finished his sentence, hysterical shrieks came from along the corridor and there was the sound of feet running.

'Miss Jenkins, there's a flood! There's water everywhere!'

Alekos gave a driven sigh. 'Where do you go for peace and quiet in this place?'

'I can't have peace and quiet—this is a school.'

A group of children ran towards them, Vivien close behind them.

'Oh, Kelly.' She looked hugely stressed and there were huge wet patches on her skirt. 'There's a flood in the girls' changing rooms. Water everywhere. It's pouring out of somewhere. Can this lot go in your room while I go to the office? We're going to have to find a plumber, or a—' she gave a helpless shrug '—I don't know who to ring. Any ideas? The whole school is going to be under water soon; maybe I should phone for a submarine. We need someone who knows about pipes and water.'

'I know about pipes and water.' Clearly exasperated, Alekos inhaled deeply. 'Where is this flood? Show me. The sooner it is solved, the sooner I can have you to myself.'

Suddenly noticing him, Vivien's eyes widened and she looked slightly stunned.

Accustomed to that reaction from women seeing Alekos for the first time, Kelly bowed to the inevitable. 'This is Alekos. Alekos, my friend and colleague, Vivien Mason.'

'Alekos?' Vivien's eyes slid questioningly to Kelly, who gave a helpless shrug.

'He's the one who bought the ring.'

'Ring?' Vivien adopted a vacant expression which might have been convincing if it hadn't been so exaggerated. 'Oh, that old thing you keep in the back of your underwear drawer? I remember it—vaguely.'

Kelly's face turned as red as a traffic light and she was horribly aware of Alekos's interested stare.

'Anyway, about this flood.' Vivien glanced over her shoulder. 'I'll call a plumber, shall I?'

Alekos was looking at the water trickling into the corridor. 'Unless he has super powers, your school will be under water before he arrives. Get me a tool box—something—whatever you have in this school,' he ordered. 'And turn off the water at the mains.' With that, he strode along the corridor, leaving Kelly gaping after him.

'Alekos, you can't.' Her eyes slid over his shockingly expensive suit and handmade shoes, and he turned his head and gave a mocking smile, reading her mind in a single glance.

'Don't judge a book by its cover—isn't that what you English say? I flew straight from meetings in Athens. Just because I'm wearing a suit, doesn't mean I can't weld a pipe. Get me something to work with, Kelly.'

'He can look that good *and* weld a pipe? Colour me bright green with envy,' Vivien murmured faintly and Kelly gave her a shove.

'Go and turn the water off.'

By the time the water was turned off and they'd located a rusty metal box of tools hidden in the caretaker's cupboard, Alekos had discovered the fault.

'The joint in this pipe has corroded.' He'd removed his jacket and his shirt was soaked, sticking to his lean, muscled torso like another skin. 'What's in that box?'

'I have no idea.' Distracted by the sheer power of his body, Kelly struggled to open the box, staggering under the weight and Alekos frowned down at the assortment of tools.

'Give me that one—no, the one underneath it; that's it.' He proceeded to remove the offending pipe and examine it closely. 'Here is your problem.' He ran his finger over a section of ancient pipe. 'I doubt it's been replaced since the school was built. Doesn't anyone maintain this place?'

Vivien was gazing at his shoulders. 'I don't think our caretaker possesses your skills. And we're a bit short of money.'

'It doesn't need much money, just regular maintenance. Kelly, my phone is in my back pocket—get it out.'

'But—'

'I have my hands rather full at the moment,' he gritted. 'Not to mention being soaking wet. If you could not choose this moment to argue, that would be appreciated.'

Kelly stepped through the water and slipped her hand into his pocket, feeling the hard muscle of his body burn through the wet fabric. Quickly, she closed her fingers around his phone and dragged it out, aware that he was as tense as she was. Four years ago she hadn't been able to keep her hands off his body—and he hadn't been able to keep his hands off hers.

It was something she'd been trying to forget ever since.

Judging from the sizzling glance he sent in her direction, he felt the same way.

Kelly gulped. 'What do you want me to do?'

'Speed dial.' He gave her instructions and she did as he said, then held the phone to his ear so that he could speak. Listening to the flow of Greek, she wished she'd spent less time focusing on his body when they were together and more time honing her language skills. At very least she should have learned how to say 'get out of my life'.

'Do you know what he's saying?' Vivien hissed and Kelly shook her head just as Alekos ended the call.

'I will have a team here in less than ten minutes.'

'A team?'

'I can fix this pipe for you, but I don't have the equipment. We need a new section of pipe, the same diameter; my security team can locate what we need and have it here. It will do them good to have something useful to do instead of hovering on street corners.' He wiped his damp forehead on his shoulder and then glanced around him in incredulity, taking in the peeling paint. 'If this place were a ship, it would have sunk by now.'

'It makes the *Titanic* look seaworthy,' Vivien agreed fervently and Kelly rolled her eyes.

Being this close to Alekos, and in these circumstances, was the worst possible torture; she didn't need to witness hero-worship from her closest friend. 'Can we just get on with this? Alekos, I'm sure there's somewhere you need to be. Now that you've identified the problem, we can sort it out, so you are free to go.'

'Go? Are you mad?' Vivien's voice was an astonished squeak. 'We're never going to be able to find anyone to fix this at such short notice. He knows what he's doing, why would you want him to go?'

'Because Kelly is feeling uncomfortable being this close to me.' A sardonic smile on his face, Alekos fixed his gaze on her. 'Isn't that right, *agape mou*?'

His use of that particular endearment sent the tension rocketing through her. It reminded her too clearly of intimate moments she was working hard to forget. 'I've changed my mind about selling the ring. I want it to go to a good home, and you're definitely not a good home. And, just because you can roll up your sleeves and fix a leaking pipe, don't think I'm impressed.'

'*I'm* impressed,' Vivien said dreamily. '*Really* impressed. I thought you ran a shipping company. But you can—wow. I mean, *wow*.'

Alekos looked amused. 'I do run a shipping company.'

'But not from behind a desk, obviously.'

'Unfortunately, it usually is from behind a desk. But I have a degree in naval architecture and marine engineering which occasionally comes in useful.' He looked up as a woman walked into the room followed by five men carrying stacks of equipment.

'These men say that—oh.' The school secretary blinked in horror and Kelly formed her lips into something approaching a smile.

'It's all under control, Janet.'

And it was. With Alekos giving orders, the men worked as an efficient team, but what really surprised her was that he did the actual work himself. His team gave him what he asked for and, while he fixed the pipe they set about cleaning up the water and setting up drying machines.

By the time Alekos had finished, a new section of pipe had replaced the old piece that had rusted away and the cloakroom was drying.

Kelly was just trying to slink away when he closed his hand around her wrist like a vice. 'No. No more running.' Hauling her against him, Alekos swung her into his arms; Kelly made a choked sound and clutched at his shoulders for support.

'Alekos! What are you doing? Put me down.'

Half-alarmed, half-laughing in envy, Vivien put a hand on his arm. 'Whatever you do, don't drop her! Gosh, if you're that desperate you can use my classroom, if you like, it's empty.'

'Put me down!' Kelly snapped, twisting in his arms. 'I want to keep the respect of these children and I won't be able to do that if you're carrying me through the school like—'

'Like a man?' Ignoring her, Alekos said something in Greek to his team and strode out of the door. 'You've put on some weight since you were nineteen.'

'Good.' Kelly banked down the hurt caused by that comment. 'I hope you put your back out.'

'It was a compliment—the extra weight appears to be distributed in all the right places, although I can't be sure without a closer inspection.'

'How can you say things like that when you're involved with another woman? You're disgusting.'

'You're jealous.'

'I'm not jealous. As far as I'm concerned, your sickeningly skinny blonde can have you.' Kelly wriggled, but wriggling just made him hold her more firmly so she lay still, trying not to breathe in his familiar male scent—*trying not to look at the dark shadow of his jaw and the impossibly long lashes.* 'Put me down right now, Alekos.'

His answer was to kiss her, and as she slipped downwards through a hazy mist of thick, swirling desire Kelly heard Vivien's envious voice coming from somewhere in the distance.

'Given the choice of him or four-million dollars, I'd choose him every time. Way to go, Kel.'

CHAPTER THREE

THE sleek black Ferrari roared along the narrow roads; Kelly was glad he'd dropped her into the seat because her legs had turned to jelly. 'I can't believe you kissed me in front of everyone. I will *never* be able to look at any of them again.'

'I thought we dealt with your inhibitions four years ago.'

'I was not inhibited! You were just always doing really embarrassing stuff that—'

'You'd never done before. I know.' He shifted gears in a smooth movement. 'I pushed it too fast, but I'd never been with anyone as inexperienced as you.' He was supremely cool and her face burned hot as a furnace.

'Well, I'm sorry!'

'Don't be. I'm Greek; teaching you was the most erotic experience of my life.'

Kelly squirmed. 'And then there was the whole thing with the lights.'

'Lights?'

'You always wanted them on!'

'I wanted to see you.'

Kelly slunk lower in her seat, remembering all the ways she'd tried to hide. 'Haven't you ever heard of global warming? We're supposed to be turning lights off. Anyway, never mind that. I'm not inhibited, but that doesn't mean I've turned into an exhibitionist. And, actually, I just don't *want* to kiss you. The thought of kissing you revolts me.'

Without taking his eyes off the road, he smiled. 'Right.'

It was the smile that flipped her over the edge—that and the fact that her pulse rate still hadn't returned to normal. 'How dare you just barge in here after four years and not even offer so much as an explanation? You're not even sorry, are you? You don't have a conscience. I could never hurt *anyone* the way you hurt me, but you just don't care.'

For a moment she thought he wasn't going to answer. His hands whitened on the wheel and his mouth compressed. 'I do have a conscience,' he said harshly. 'That's why I didn't marry you. It would have been wrong.'

'*What?* What sort of twisted logic is that? Oh, never mind.' Kelly closed her eyes, completely humiliated. She'd kissed him back—hungrily, desperately, foolishly. 'Why *did* you kiss me, anyway?'

He shifted gears again, his hand strong and steady. 'Because you wouldn't stop talking.'

Kelly's ego shrivelled still further; it was not because she was irresistible or because he just couldn't help himself. He'd kissed her as a method of shutting her up. 'Slow down. I get car sick.' Not for anything would she admit that the kiss had made her dizzy. Alekos knew everything there was to know about kissing a woman, which was just her bad luck, she thought gloomily. Staring out of the window as trees flashed past, she wondered what he'd meant by that comment.

Why had his conscience stopped him from marrying her—because it wouldn't have been fair to deprive all those other women of great sex?

She swallowed down a hysterical laugh.

It was almost worth tearing the ring from round her neck just to make this whole thing end. What did she have left to lose? Only her pride. And Alekos wasn't stupid. He probably knew exactly how she felt about him.

She wished now she hadn't given him the address of her cottage, but she'd been so embarrassed by the exhibition he'd created at the school that she'd just wanted to escape.

Her heart pounding, her mouth dry, Kelly tried to think clearly, but it was impossible to think, jammed into this enclosed space with him. The length of his powerful thigh was too close to hers, and every time she risked looking at him the memories came flooding back: his firm, sensual mouth brushing hers, proving to her that she'd never properly been kissed before; his strong, clever hands teaching her what her body could do, stripping away her inhibitions, everything so shockingly intense and exquisitely perfect that she'd felt like the luckiest woman on the planet.

But their relationship had been more than just incredible sex.

It had been laughter and an astonishing chemistry. It had been *fun*.

It had been the most stimulating relationship she'd ever had, before or since.

And the most painful.

There had been moments when she'd thought that losing him would be the end of her—standing there, waiting for a man who didn't turn up. Trying to pretend it didn't matter.

Transported straight back to her childhood, Kelly closed her eyes and reminded herself that it was different. The trouble was that rejection felt pretty much the same, no matter who was responsible.

'Take the next left,' she said huskily. 'I live in the pink cottage with the rusty gate. You can park outside. I'll get you the ring and you can go.'

This was a good test of how she was doing, she told herself. If the only way she could handle her feelings for Alekos was by not seeing him, then what had the past four years been about? Why invest so much time on rebuilding a life so carefully if it could be that vulnerable?

She'd got over him, hadn't she? She'd moved on. Apart from the occasionally disturbing dream involving a virile Greek man and incredible sex, she no longer ached and yearned. Yes, she wore the ring around her neck, but that was going to change. Once she handed it over she was going to do something radical, like joining a project to build a school in Africa or something. And she was going to kiss loads of men until she found someone else who knew how to do it properly. He couldn't be the only person.

Noticing the neighbour's curtains twitching, Kelly groaned. She was giving everyone enough to gossip about for at least two lifetimes. 'Don't you *dare* kiss me here. Mrs Hill is ninety-six and she watches from the window. You'll give her a heart attack.'

Climbing out of the car, she glanced dubiously at Alekos, wondering how he always managed to look completely at home in his surroundings. Boardroom or beach, city or tiny village, he was confident in himself, and it showed. He stood outside her house, the early-evening sunlight glinting off his dark hair, his face so extraordinarily handsome that it took her breath away. Four years had simply added to his raw sex appeal, adding breadth to his shoulders and a hardness to his features that had been missing before.

'This is where you live?'

Kelly bristled. 'We're not all millionaires,' she muttered. 'And it's very bad-mannered of you to look down your nose.'

'I'm *not* looking down my nose.' He shot her an impatient look. 'Stop being so sensitive and stop imagining what I'm thinking because, believe me, you don't have a clue. I'm just surprised, that's all. It's really quiet here, and you are a very sociable person. I imagined you living in London and going to parties every night.'

Not wanting to flatter his ego by revealing what a mess she'd been after he'd left, Kelly fumbled in her bag for her keys. 'I am out every night. You'd be surprised.'

He glanced around him, one eyebrow lifted. 'You're right. I'd be very surprised. Are you trying to tell me this place comes alive at midnight?'

Kelly thought of the badgers, foxes and hedgehogs that invaded her garden. 'It's really lively. There's a sort of underground nightlife.' It came to something, she thought gloomily, when badgers had a more interesting sex life than you did. But that was partly her fault, wasn't it? After the press had torn her apart, she'd hidden away. 'Wait there; I'll bring you the ring.'

'I'll come in with you. I'd hate to give your neighbour a heart attack, and we're attracting too much attention out here.'

Her eyes slid from his powerful shoulders to his hard jaw and she looked away quickly, her stomach churning. The thought of him in her little cottage made her heart-rate double. 'I don't want you in my home, Alekos.'

His answer to that was to remove the keys from her hand and stride towards her front door.

Enraged, Kelly sprinted after him. 'Don't you *dare* go into my house without invitation!'

'There's a simple solution to that: invite me.'

'I will not. I only invite nice people into my home, and you—' she stabbed his chest with her finger '—are definitely not a nice person.'

'Why did you sell my ring?'

'Why did you leave me on our wedding day?'

He inhaled sharply. 'I've told you.'

'You were doing me a favour—yes, I heard you. You have a warped sense of what constitutes generous behaviour.'

For once he seemed to be struggling to find the right words. 'It was difficult for me.'

'Tell me about it. On second thoughts, don't bother. I don't even want to know.' Kelly decided that she couldn't bear to hear him list all the reasons she was wrong for him. *Couldn't bear to hear him compare her to the skinny, sophisticated blonde she'd seen in the magazine.* 'Come in, if you must. I'll get the ring and then you can go.'

He stood still, immovable. 'I know I hurt you—'

'Gosh, you're quick, I'll give you that.' Kelly snatched the keys back from him and opened her door. She wished he'd just give up and go away, but Alekos didn't give up, did he? It was that unstoppable tenacity that had made him into the rich, powerful man he was. He didn't see obstacles; he had a goal and he pursued it, ploughing down everything in his path if necessary. Yet he was praised as a truly innovative businessman with inspirational leadership-skills. And as for his skills as a lover...

Refusing to think about that, Kelly pushed open her front door, wincing slightly as the door jammed on a pile of magazines. 'Sorry.' She shoved at the door. 'I've been trying to throw them away.'

'Trying?'

Kelly stiffened defensively. 'I find it hard, throwing things away. I'm always scared I'll get rid of something I might want.' Stooping, she gathered the magazines, looked hesitantly at the recycling box and then put them back down on the floor. 'And some of these magazines have some really interesting articles I might want to read again some day.'

Alekos was looking at her intently, as if she were a fascinating creature from another planet. 'You always did drop everything where you stood.' The faint amusement in his eyes was the final straw.

'Yes, well, none of us are perfect, and at least I don't deliberately try and hurt people,' Kelly snapped—then gasped in horror as he smacked his forehead hard on the doorframe. 'Oh—mind out! Poor you—are you OK? Are you hurt? I'll get you some ice.' Sympathy bubbled over until she remembered she wasn't supposed to feel sympathy for this man. 'These cottages are old. You need to bend your head coming through there.'

Rubbing his fingers over his bronzed forehead, he grimaced. 'You need to warn people *before* they knock themselves unconscious.'

'It's not a problem for anyone under six foot.'

'I'm six-three.'

She didn't need reminding. He towered over her, all broad shoulders and pumping testosterone.

Unsettled, Kelly took a step backwards. 'Yes, well, you should have been looking where you were going.'

'I was looking at *you*.' His irritable tone implied he was less than pleased about that fact, but for some reason his reluctant confession really cheered her up.

The fact that she could still make this man miss his step gave her a ridiculous sense of feminine satisfaction. Maybe she wasn't thin and blonde, but he still noticed her whether he wanted to or not.

But satisfaction was short lived as she realised his wide shoulders virtually filled the hallway. Sexual awareness and a cloying, dangerous heat spread through her cosy cottage. Trapping a man like Alekos in this confined space was like putting a tiger in a small cage: fine if you were on the other side of the wire.

Frightened by how quickly her composure was deserting her, Kelly dumped her keys on a pile of unopened letters, wondering why being with him instantly made her think of sex. Their relationship hadn't just been about sex, so why was she suddenly thinking about nothing but it?

Probably because her sex life had been so unfulfilling since they had parted, she thought wistfully. Suddenly she wished she hadn't been so choosy over the last few years. If she'd had an active sex life, maybe she wouldn't be feeling this way.

Maybe that nagging ache wouldn't be present.

The truth was she'd poured her energies into her teaching, ignoring that other side of herself, pretending that it didn't exist.

BARBARA HANNAY

A Miracle for His Secret Son

Freya and Gus shared a perfect summer, until
Gus left town for a future that couldn't include
Freya.... Now eleven years on, Freya has a life-
changing revelation for Gus: they have a son,
Nick, who needs a new kidney—a gift only his
father can provide. Gus is stunned by the news,
but vows to help Nick. And despite everything,
Gus realizes that he still loves Freya.

**Can they forge a future together and
give Nick another miracle...a family?**

Available October 2010

www.eHarlequin.com

HR17688

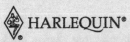

as he struggled with the word. 'But it didn't occur to me. We didn't—I mean, we *did*, but it was just the once. That time on your kitchen table.'

Kelly flinched. 'Romantic, wasn't it?' Her sarcasm was met by taut silence and then he cleared his throat.

'I made you pregnant on that one occasion?'

'So it would seem. Let's hope our child never asks how, or where, he was conceived.'

He dragged his hand over the back of his neck. 'I assumed you were using contraception.'

'Well, I wasn't. Pass me those shoes, please.'

'Shoes?' Distracted, Alekos followed the direction of her finger and retrieved a pair of abandoned fuschia-pink stilettos from under the bed. 'You shouldn't wear those with your problem with walking.'

'I don't have a problem with walking.' Kelly opened the case gingerly and fed the shoes in one by one, trying not to let any of the contents escape. 'I have a problem with your floor.'

'Why weren't you using contraception?' Dark lashes lowered over his eyes as he focused on the part of the conversation that interested him.

'Because I didn't need it. It seems I'm genetically programmed to give myself only to the lower forms of life. If there's a decent, honest, family-loving man around, I go blind. Now you can go and beat your chest and do all the other things you cave-dweller, alpha males do.' Kelly was about to reach for her case again when a strong, brown hand covered hers. She stared at his hand and swallowed. 'Don't touch me. What do you think you're doing?'

'I'm doing the things we cave-dweller, alpha males do,' he drawled. 'Like lifting heavy weights. If you want it lifted, I'll lift it.'

'It's a suitcase, not a piece of fallen masonry. I can manage.'

'I don't want you to do anything which will harm the baby.'

'*My* baby. *My* baby, Alekos! Stop calling it *the* baby. What if it can hear you?' The tension exploded inside her, punctured by fears she'd been afraid to express even to herself. 'What if it *knows* you don't want it?'

There was a long silence during which he watched her with an intensity that made her heart race.

'Don't ever say that,' he said thickly. 'All right, I'm the first to admit that this wasn't what I wanted—I wouldn't have chosen this to happen—but it's happened and it's my responsibility. I'm not walking away from that.'

'Forget it. I don't want to drag you along behind the pram like some sort of prisoner of war. I'd rather do this by myself.'

'*Theé mou*, I'm being honest, Kelly! That is what you wanted, isn't it? If I said to you, yes, I'm thrilled about this baby, would you believe me?'

Choking back tears, Kelly bit her lip. 'No.'

'Exactly. I am telling you how I'm truly feeling. This has been a shock.' The disordered mess of his usually smooth hair was an indication of how much of a shock. 'But I will sort myself out. There is no way I would ever leave the baby without a father.'

'*My* baby!' Kelly yelled, putting her hands over her stomach protectively. 'If you call it *the* baby again, I'll punch you.'

Alekos drew in an unsteady breath. 'How about *our* baby?' he said hoarsely, and something unfamiliar glittered in his eyes as he stared down at her flat stomach. 'How does *our* baby sound to you?'

'It sounds like a particularly tasteless joke.' Not even allowing herself to go there, Kelly reached for the phone. 'How do I buy a ticket on a plane? I need basic Greek.'

Alekos's response to that was to gently prise the phone out of her fingers. 'You have a basic Greek,' he said dryly. 'Me. And I have no idea how to buy a ticket on a plane. I've never bought one. And neither will you. You're going to stay here until we work this out. And *stop* talking about leaving. If the baby can hear you, then he will be feeling really unsettled by now.'

'What is there to work out? I'm pregnant and you don't want children, no matter how much you kid yourself you'll do the right thing. Why don't you want children, anyway?' Exhausted by the dilemma in which she found herself, Kelly shot him an exasperated look. 'Is your ego really that fragile? What sort of selfish, self-absorbed, playboy billionaire are you that you can't even bring yourself to be out of the limelight long enough to have a child?'

Alekos looked at her, his face surprisingly pale, his magnificent bone structure highlighted by the sudden tension that gripped him. 'The sort who knows exactly how it feels to come second to a selfish, self-absorbed father,' he said flatly. 'The sort who vowed never, ever to mess up a child's life. The sort who lived through hell.'

Breathe, breathe, Kelly said to herself, wishing Vivien were here waving a paper bag at her.

Still stunned by Alekos's confession, she was now completely torn, her plan to get on a plane and fly home blown to the wind by his totally unexpected revelation about his own childhood.

Yet staying didn't make sense, did it?

If ever a relationship was doomed, it was theirs.

But the memory of his strained features was stuck in her head. And those words: *the sort who vowed never, ever to mess up a child's life.*

Torn, she sat for a minute, telling herself that all that mattered was the baby. She had to put the baby first. And yet…

'Oh, for crying out loud.' Kelly removed her shoes and walked barefoot across the tiled floor, where she'd slipped, and out on to the terrace. He'd said that if she wanted to talk he'd be outside.

Fine, they could talk—for five minutes. She'd just check he was all right and then she'd leave.

Her feet made no sound on the terrace and Kelly stood for a moment, puzzled, because there was no sign of him.

Then she heard a splash from the pool.

Glancing in that direction, she watched as Alekos powered his way across the pool, water streaming off his muscular shoulders as he swam, clearly trying to work off his frustration as he cut through the water with explosive force.

His body pulsated with strength and power, and Kelly gave a little shiver, remembering how it felt when all that power and passion was focused on her. Refusing to join him in the pool, she gritted her teeth and sat down on the edge of a sun lounger to wait.

The view was stunning, stretching across the gardens and down to the perfect blue sea. Normally the peace and tranquillity of her surroundings would have calmed her, but she was incapable of feeling calm in the current situation, with Alekos still within her line of vision.

Having swum endless punishing lengths, Alekos sprang from the pool, swept water from his face with his hand and prowled over to her.

Kelly slid back on the seat. 'That's close enough. I—I just came to check you're OK.'

'Why wouldn't I be OK?'

'Because you—you talked about stuff you don't usually talk about.' Out of her depth, she looked at him warily. 'I just wanted to make sure you're all right.'

He gave a wry smile and reached for a towel. 'Typical Kelly,' he said softly. 'You hate me, but you think I might be upset so you have to check I'm all right.'

'I just don't want your death on my conscience.' Finding it impossible to concentrate with all that gleaming male muscle on display, Kelly averted her eyes. 'So, let me just check I've understood this correctly: you're basically saying that you don't want children because you're afraid you'll hurt them, is that right?'

'Yes.'

Kelly chewed her lip, waiting for a full confession to spill out. When he was silent, she prompted him. 'Your dad was selfish? He hurt you?'

'Yes.'

Kelly stared at him in exasperation. 'Can't you say more than "yes"? "Yes" doesn't tell me anything about your feelings. Oh, forget it,' she mumbled. 'You don't want to talk about it, I get that. Whatever it is, you've blocked it out. I heard what you said to the doctor, although I didn't realise at the time what it meant. You'd rather just plough on, pretending it didn't happen, because that's what works for you. The trouble is, that doesn't work for me. I played guessing games last time

and I guessed all wrong. I assumed you'd just decided you didn't want me—that I was too inexperienced or something.'

'I loved the fact you were inexperienced.' He knotted the towel around his hips and Kelly swallowed, trying to focus on a different part of him.

'Right. Which just goes to show I'm rubbish at reading your mind. And you won't tell me what's on your mind, so we might as well give up.'

'We are not giving up. But you're right—it is a subject I find hard to talk about.' He poured himself a glass of water from the jug that had been left on the table. 'What is it you want to know?'

'Well, all of it! I want to understand.'

Alekos stared into the glass in his hand. 'My parents had a disastrous marriage. My mother had an affair, my father left her, I was made to choose who I wanted to live with.' He lifted the glass to his lips and drank while Kelly stared at him, absorbing that information slowly, slotting the pieces together in her brain.

'Y-you were made to choose between the two of them?' Shaken, she rubbed her hand over her forehead. 'But—how old were you?'

'I was six. They stood me in a room and asked me who I wanted to live with. I knew that whichever decision I made, it would be the wrong one for them.' His tone grim, Alekos thumped the glass down on the table. 'I chose to live with my mother. I was worried about what she might do if I went to live with my father. She was the more vulnerable of the two of them. She told me that if she lost me she'd die. No six-year-old boy wants his mother to die.'

Six? They'd forced a six-year-old to choose who he wanted to live with? Kelly was appalled. 'That's completely shocking. What about your dad? Didn't he understand what a hideous position you were in?'

His mouth twisted. 'A son is a Greek man's most precious possession. To him, I made the wrong choice. He never forgave me.'

'But—'

'I ceased to exist. I never saw him again.' Alekos looked at her and for once there was no mockery in his eyes, no hint of humour. Just a hard, steely determination. 'I never, ever want any action of mine to hurt a child. And it happens. All too easily. So now you understand why I overreacted to the revelation that you want at least four children. It came as a shock.'

Kelly licked her lips. 'I wish you'd told me.'

'We weren't doing that much talking, were we? Most of our communication was physical.' He gave a cynical laugh. 'To call our relationship a whirlwind would be like calling Mount Everest a molehill.'

'I did plenty of talking,' Kelly muttered, feeling a sudden stab of guilt. She'd never asked him that much about himself, had she? She'd never pushed him to talk about his family or his hopes. She'd been thinking about her dreams, not his. 'It didn't occur to me you were thinking that way. You just seemed so confident about everything. You seemed to know exactly what you wanted.'

'I did know what I wanted. Or, at least, I thought I did.' Alekos pulled her to her feet and drew her towards him. 'Things change. Life throws things at you that you weren't expecting.'

Without her shoes, she barely reached his shoulder. For a brief, indulgent moment Kelly leaned her forehead

against smooth, bronzed skin, breathing in the tantalising scent of him. 'Yes, life does throw the unexpected. This doesn't feel like the fairy tale.'

He gave a cynical laugh. 'Some of those fairy tales were pretty nasty, *agape mou*. How about the wicked witch and the fairy godmother?'

'The fairy godmother was good. You mean the wicked stepmother.'

'Her too. I told you I'd make a terrible father; I don't even know the right stories,' Alekos lifted her chin with strong fingers. 'How is your poor head?'

'Aching. Like the rest of me. I feel as though I've been trampled by a herd of cows. I'm never wearing shoes in your house again.' But the thing that ached most was her heart—for him. For the small child who had been forced to make an impossible choice by parents too selfishly absorbed by their own problems to put him first. And for herself, who now had to make an equally impossible choice.

Leave and live without him, or stay and risk that he'd walk away again?

She had no idea what to do, which decision to make.

Alekos drew his thumb slowly over her lower lip. 'You're never wearing shoes again? How about clothes?' His voice was husky. 'Perhaps you'd better not wear those, either.'

'Don't. I can't think when you do that.' Kelly tried to pull away but he held her firmly, his hand warm against her back. 'I'm completely and utterly confused now. I always thought you were a totally together, sorted-out person.'

'I am in my business life,' Alekos drawled, sliding his hand into her hair and trailing his mouth along her

jaw. 'It's just in my personal life I manage to mess up in spectacular fashion.' This surprisingly honest admission disabled her pathetic attempt to resist him.

She felt impossibly torn.

'We can't get back together for the sake of a baby you never wanted.'

He cupped her face in his hands and brought his mouth down on hers.

'I brought you here *before* I knew you were pregnant.'

'If you were that keen on mending fences, why didn't you come back to England?'

'Because in England it rains even in July, and here in Corfu I can guarantee that you will be walking round in a bikini.' His eyes gleamed dark with the promise of seduction. 'Or less. I'm that shallow.'

'It can't be all about the sex, Alekos!' Her hand slid to the hard muscle of his shoulders and she pushed him away. 'Having sex is the easy part. It's the relationship bit that's the hard bit.'

'I know that.'

'You don't want a baby. I don't see a solution.' But she wanted one badly. *So badly.*

'We'll find one together.' He took her mouth then, plundering the depths with skilled strokes of his tongue, stirring up emotions she'd struggled to keep under control. His hard body pressed against hers and the flat of his hand kept them welded together while his mouth created a storm of passion.

Kelly melted into him.

He was the only man who'd ever been able to do this to her. The only man who could make her act against her better judgement.

He groaned something in Greek against her mouth, then switched to English. 'For weeks I have wanted to do this—since that time in your kitchen I have thought of nothing else. You have been driving me wild, *erota mou*.'

Kelly lifted her hands, speared his hair with her fingers and let herself go. The taste of him was so dangerously good that she gave a low moan. The sun beat down on their heads and the birds flew playfully across the surface of the pool, but neither of them noticed, so intent were they on each other.

It was the sound of a door slamming close by that caused them to break apart.

Kelly gasped. 'Y-you're just confusing me.'

'There's nothing confusing about it.' Alekos had his hand behind her head and he drew her mouth to his again. 'You want this as much as I do.' The air was humid, thick with sexual tension, and like a drowning person being swept downstream Kelly struggled to keep her head above the water.

'Four years ago you really hurt me.'

'I know.'

'You didn't even explain.' She was looking at his mouth so close to hers, at the sensual curve of his lips and the dark shadow of his jaw. 'You were really horrid.'

'I know that too; I was a real bleep.' His voice was husky and his black lashes shielded eyes that smouldered with the promise of sex. 'I can make it up to you. I can make this work. We can find a way.'

'I don't see how. Don't you *dare* kiss me again, Alekos—don't you dare—not until I tell you it's OK.'

Kelly tried to pull away but he was stronger than her and he wasn't afraid to use that strength when it suited him.

His kiss was a devastating reminder of what they shared: power play. 'You are going to forgive me, *agape mou*,' he murmured, taking her lower lip gently between his teeth. 'You are angry, I know, but that is good because it shows you still care.'

'It shows that I have more sense than to let you back into my life again.' But the words lacked conviction, not just because that brief kiss had left her weak and shaking, but also because of the baby. She didn't want to just walk away, did she? It wasn't that simple. But if she stayed there was a strong chance that he'd hurt her again, and this time he'd be hurting their baby too. 'I can't do this, Alekos. I can't put myself through that again. I can't risk it.'

He cupped her face in his hands. 'You want me, you know you do.'

'No, actually, I don't know that at all.' She struggled against her feelings. 'It's just a physical thing.'

'If you don't want me, and it's just a physical thing, why have you been wearing my ring around your neck for four years?'

Kelly's eyes flew wide. 'Who told you that?'

'I saw it after we made love in your kitchen,' he said huskily, brushing his mouth over hers. 'I didn't know you'd been wearing it for four years. That was a guess that you just confirmed. But you have to admit that it says something.'

'It says that you're devious.'

'It says that what we shared has never gone away.' He leaned his forehead against hers. 'Stay, Kelly. Stay, *agape mou*.'

'No, because I can't think straight when I'm near you, and I need to decide what to do without being influenced,' Kelly moaned, turning her head away. 'I'm pregnant, Alekos, and you don't want children. So, tell me how this can ever work! Or are you suddenly going to pretend you've discovered this is what you've always wanted?'

He breathed out slowly. 'No, I'm not pretending that. But it's happened. That changes things. I admit that hearing about the baby is a shock, but we will work it out.'

'How?'

'I don't know.' He was brutally honest. 'I need some time to get used to the idea. But, in the meantime, you leaving won't help the situation.'

'If I stay, we'll just end up in bed, and that won't help the situation either.' Ripped apart with indecision, Kelly stared at him. 'Last time it was all about the sex. You said that yourself. If I stay, then it has to be different.'

'Different in what way?'

'It has to be about the whole relationship.' She pulled away from him and stared at her suitcase. She didn't know what to do. And the only person she could talk it through with was the same person who made it an impossible decision. If his desire not to have children was so deep rooted that he'd left her on her wedding day, that wasn't going to change, was it?

On the other hand, it was impossible not to admire the fact that he was still standing here. That took courage, didn't it? That showed he was serious about trying to make it work.

Unless it really was all about the sex.

There was only one way to challenge that possibility.

'We'll sleep in separate bedrooms,' she blurted out impulsively and his eyes flared dark with shock.

'Fine,' he said tightly. 'Separate bedrooms. If that's what you want.'

Astounded that he'd agreed so readily, Kelly didn't know whether to be impressed or disappointed. *Was it what she wanted?* She wasn't sure, but now that she'd suggested it she had to follow through. '*And* you have to tell me what you're thinking. All the time. I want to know, because I'm obviously not good at reading your mind and it's exhausting trying to guess.'

His gaze slid over her. 'You're hot, and you should get out of your clothes. I want you naked.'

Feeling as though she was boiling inside, Kelly glared at him in exasperation. 'I'm trying to have a proper conversation! Do you think you could possibly think about something other than sex for a moment?'

'You told me to tell you what I'm thinking,' he said silkily. 'That's what I was thinking.'

Kelly's face burned. 'In that case, I want you to censor your thoughts. I don't want to hear the ones that involve sex.'

'Censor my thoughts.' Alekos arched an eyebrow and his eyes gleamed with sardonic humour. 'So you want me to tell you everything I'm thinking, as long as it's what you *want* me to be thinking. This is complicated, isn't it?'

'You built a billion-dollar business from nothing but a rowing boat,' Kelly said stiffly. 'I'm sure you can rise to the challenge if you really want to. And now I'm going to unpack my case.'

'The staff will do that.'

'I'd rather do it myself.' She needed an excuse to have a few minutes without him looking at her. She needed to think, and she couldn't do that when he was standing this close.

A faint smile touched his mouth. 'Why not just tip the contents of the case over the floor and have done with it?'

'You may think I'm messy, but I happen to think you're far too uptight and controlling.' Flying into defence mode, Kelly lifted her chin. 'There's something suspicious about someone who needs everything in their life to be neatly ordered. Spontaneity can be a healthy thing. You might want to remember that.'

And *she* needed to try and remember why on earth she'd thought it would be a good idea to suggest separate bedrooms.

Kelly stalked back inside the villa, wishing she had more control over her mouth.

She'd just consigned herself to endless sleepless nights. If he was going to talk about sex all the time, the days weren't looking too restful either.

CHAPTER SIX

'So, WHERE exactly are we going tonight?' Kelly lay on a sun lounger next to the pool, sipping lemonade with no bits, trying not to think about sex.

Why was it, she wondered gloomily, that when you knew you couldn't have something you just thought about it all the time?

And why was it that Alekos, who usually crashed straight through any decision he didn't like, had accepted this one without argument?

Not that she could accuse him of not being attentive. Over the past few weeks, he had apparently expressed every thought in his head, some of them so hot that she'd been relieved they were on their own in the villa. He'd also presented her with flowers, jewellery, a book he thought she'd enjoy and a new iPod to replace the one she'd accidently dropped in the pool—but he hadn't touched her. Not once.

And not once had he challenged her request for separate bedrooms.

'We're flying to Athens.' Apparently oblivious to the fact that she was reaching boiling point, he scrolled through the messages on his BlackBerry, occasionally typing in a response. His cool, relaxed demeanour was in direct contrast to her own increasing stress levels.

Kelly was agonisingly aware of him.

It didn't help that he'd chosen to sit on the edge of her sun lounger, as close to her as possible without touching. Sneaking a look at him, she felt a sharp dart of desire pierce her body. Her eyes slid to his muscular legs and her belly clenched.

Was he doing it on purpose, sitting this close?

She pulled her knees up, worried that her thighs would look fat pressed against the sun lounger.

The fact that he was spending so much time with her, surprised her. Over the past couple of weeks he'd only left her side a couple of times, to attend meetings in Athens that couldn't be conducted on the phone. Apart from that, they'd been together at the villa, and the fact that he'd made that compromise for her had Kelly even more confused.

It was a big sacrifice for a guy like Alekos who was completely driven in his work and constantly in demand. The fact that he was making such huge adjustments in his schedule for her was incredibly flattering. In fact it would have been all too easy to fall back into their old relationship with no thought. Every minute of the day, she had to remind herself to be wary.

Living together was becoming all too intense, she thought to herself, watching him lean forward, transfixed by the ripple of muscle and display of strength. It was all too intense. It was a good thing they were going out.

'Is this a date or something?' Horribly conscious of him, Kelly wished she hadn't risked the bikini. It drew his gaze, and his smouldering, sizzling attention was sending her hormones screaming into the danger zone.

His gaze lingered on hers and then his sensual mouth curved into a smile. 'More of a business dinner than a date. I want you with me tonight.'

The words made Kelly's insides soften to pulp. He wanted her with him. He was including her in his life. He was sharing things with her.

Their relationship was progressing. Obviously it *had* been a good idea to suggest separate bedrooms. She shifted slightly on the sun lounger, wishing that denying herself didn't feel quite so difficult. The chemistry between them was electric. Even without touching him she could feel the tension in his muscles. She was experiencing the same tension. By imposing bedroom limits all she'd done was increase the sexual temperature around them to dangerous levels.

'This meeting—' she curled her legs up so that there was less chance of brushing against him '—tell me what I'm supposed to say. I don't want to say or do the wrong thing.'

'I am not expecting you to close a deal,' Alekos said dryly. 'Just to be yourself.'

'What do I have to wear? Will it be smart?'

'Very. I have already arranged a selection of clothes to be taken to our Athens home so that you can choose something you like.'

Our Athens home.

The words made the breath catch in her throat and Kelly allowed a little flame of hope to bloom inside her. Would he be talking about 'our' home if he was planning to walk out on her again? No. He was talking as if they were a couple. A partnership.

The fact that she'd never heard him talk like that before raised her spirits, and she sat patiently while he took phone call after phone call, some in English, some in Greek.

Determined not to be impressed by the influence he wielded, Kelly pondered the evening ahead. 'So, how long are we spending in Athens?'

'Just one night. My pilot is picking us up in an hour.'

'An *hour*?' Losing her pretence at cool, Kelly sat upright in a flash of panic. 'I have one *hour* to get ready to go and meet a load of people I'm supposed to impress? That's all?'

'I'm the only person you have to impress,' he said smoothly. 'And I assumed you would get ready when we arrive in Athens. I have arranged for some people to help you.'

'What sort of people?' Torn between relief and outrage, Kelly frowned at him. 'A plastic surgeon?'

'*Not* a plastic surgeon. I don't think you're in need of one of those.' There was laughter in his eyes. 'A stylist and a hairdresser.'

'Stylist? I'm not in need of a plastic surgeon but I *am* in need of a stylist?' Her confidence punctured, Kelly pushed her hair behind her ear. 'Are you saying you don't like my style?'

He sighed. 'I love your style. But most women consider that sort of thing a treat.' His smile faded and his eyes narrowed warily. 'Did I get it wrong? Because I can cancel.'

'No,' Kelly said hurriedly, 'Don't cancel. It might be quite—' she shrugged '—fun, I suppose. Maybe they'll give me one of those seaweed-wrap things that makes you lose a stone in five minutes.'

'If they do that, then they'll never work for me again. Why are women always so incredibly conscious about their weight?'

'Because men are incredibly shallow,' Kelly said with dignity, swinging her legs off the sun lounger.

'Where are you going?'

She picked up her sunglasses and her book. 'I'm going to get ready.'

'You can get ready when we arrive at Athens.'

'I'm getting ready to get ready. I can't face a stylist looking like this.'

Clearly out of his depth, Alekos dug his hand into his hair. 'I will *never* understand women.'

'Stick at it. You're a bright man; you'll get there eventually.'

His house was in the smartest district of Athens, tucked away from the other mansions and hidden at the end of a long, winding drive.

Approaching from the air, Kelly felt slightly faint.

It was huge. Beneath her she could see the architecturally beautiful villa with its wide terrace facing over the city of Athens. An ancient vine offered shade, and water cascaded over a series of stones and into an incredible swimming pool. It was a smooth curve, an oasis of clear, turquoise water framed by tumbling bougainvillea and hot-pink oleander.

Kelly thought of her tiny rented cottage in Little Molting. When she stood in her kitchen, she could almost touch all four walls. This was another world.

Feeling overwhelmed and more than a little intimidated, she clutched her seat as the helicopter settled on a circular pad a little distance from the villa.

Four powerfully built men immediately came into view.

Kelly lifted her eyebrows. 'Who are they?'

'Part of my security team.'

'Is there something you're not telling me?'

'In Athens I am more careful,' Alekos said shortly, unclipping her seat belt and urging her towards the door. 'Wealth makes you a kidnap target. I want to be able to get on with my work without looking over my shoulder.'

Kelly was affronted on his behalf. She knew his ever-expanding business had created literally thousands of jobs, many of which went to Greeks. She knew him to be fiercely patriotic, supporting local charities and numerous good causes. It was one of the things she'd loved about him when they'd first met.

Following him along the path and into the villa, it was impossible not to stare because it was, without doubt, the most impressive home she'd ever seen. When they'd been together before, they'd spent all their time at his villa in Corfu, so she'd never seen his main residence.

Acres of costly marble and glass gave a sleek, contemporary feel to the place. Beautiful artwork added splashes of colour to the white walls; the furnishings were simple and elegant but the overall feel was one of incredible wealth and privilege. All of it a million miles from her own incredibly ordinary background.

'We don't have much time.' Without breaking stride, Alekos led her up a wide staircase and pushed open a door. 'The staff are all waiting to help you. I will leave you to get ready.'

'But—' Kelly had a million questions she wanted to ask, but he was already striding away from her, his mobile in his hand as he fielded yet another phone call.

Humbled and frustrated by the constant demands on his attention, she stood there feeling like an intruder.

'Miss Jenkins?' A woman hurried across the room towards her, her black hair caught up in an elegant knot at the base of her neck. 'I'm Helen. If we could make a start?'

Relieved to have a purpose, Kelly followed her into a suite of rooms and stared in disbelief at the racks of clothes in front of her. It was as if an exclusive store had been opened up for her use alone. In the short time she'd spent with Alekos four years ago, she'd never seen this side of his life. They'd spent time walking barefoot on the beach; they'd shared dinner on the terrace of his villa wearing the same clothes they'd worn to visit a local market.

Now his life was laid out in front of her.

Two other women were hovering but it was obvious that it was Helen who was in charge. 'If we could start by choosing the dress, Miss Jenkins, then we can decide on hair and make-up.' Her eyes narrowed, she studied Kelly and then walked briskly to the rails. 'I think I have something that would be perfect.'

Kelly, who had been worrying about exactly what constituted 'perfect' for a business dinner, stared as the woman whisked a dress off the rail. 'Hot pink?'

'You will look spectacular. Colours of the Mediterranean.' Helen slipped the dress off the hanger. 'Your eyes are the colour of the sea, your hair the colour of washed sand and this dress—' she shrugged '—is the colour of oleander. Do you like it?'

Kelly stared at the mouth-watering silk confection on the hanger. 'I'm trying to look grown-up and sophisticated—I thought maybe something safe. Something black?'

The woman gave her a pitying smile. 'Black is for funerals. I was told that tonight is a celebration. Why don't you slide into the bath that Nina has prepared for you and then we'll try this for a change. If you don't like it, we'll find something else.'

A celebration?

Kelly's heart fluttered. As she slid into scented water in the largest bath-tub she'd ever seen, she wondered exactly what they were going to be celebrating.

It must be something big if Alekos was going to all this trouble.

And he'd wanted her here, which meant it couldn't be business-related or he would have done that on his own.

It must be about *them*, she thought to herself with a shiver of excitement. Over the past few weeks they hadn't really discussed the future; they'd been concentrating more on the present and their relationship. Which was good, she told herself. That was the right way to do it.

And if a small part of her was slightly disappointed that Alekos hadn't mentioned the baby, then another part of her understood. This was a big thing for him, wasn't it? And he was nothing like her; he didn't deal with problems publicly. He worked them out quietly for himself.

She needed to be patient and give him time.

The fact that he'd brought her here proved that he saw them as a couple. She was part of his life now.

Reflecting on the likely nature of the forthcoming 'celebration', Kelly trailed her fingers through the frothy, scented bubbles. Obviously they were going to be celebrating something that hadn't happened yet.

Her heart gave a spring and she felt a flutter of excitement.

Was he going to propose?

She racked her brains to think of other reasons to celebrate, but nothing came to mind. Exams, new jobs: it couldn't be any of those things.

Lying in the warm water, Kelly tried to work out whether she'd say yes straight away or make him wait.

But why make him wait? What would be the point of that? She loved him—she'd never stopped loving him— and now she was having his child. It was a pointless waste of time pretending that she didn't want to be with him.

Her excitement levels rose to almost agonising proportions, and Kelly could barely sit still as one of the girls washed and conditioned her hair.

'I dare not do too much to it or I will be in trouble with the boss.' Helen trimmed it and then blow dried it into soft waves. 'He is right that you have beautiful hair.'

'Alekos said that?'

'"I need her to stun the crowd, Helen",' Helen parroted as she repeated her instructions from Alekos. '"But don't touch her hair. She has beautiful hair. And, whatever you do, don't cut it short or you will never work for me again".'

Taking the fact that she had to stun a crowd to be yet more evidence that he was introducing her to the world as someone important in his life, Kelly beamed. 'You work for him a lot?'

Helen smiled and reached for the make-up she'd already spread across the table. 'He used to fly me to Corfu to blow dry his grandmother's hair. She always loved to look her best, but she found it harder and harder to travel because of her health, so Alekos took me to her. He adored her.'

'Oh.' Surprised by that revelation, Kelly realised that Alekos had rarely mentioned his grandmother. 'I never knew her. She died before I met him. He told me that the Corfu villa was once hers.'

The doctor's words flew into her head.

I remember you coming here to stay with your grandmother as a child. I remember one summer in particular, when you were six years old. You didn't speak for a month. You had suffered a terrible trauma.

Corfu had been his sanctuary, she realised as she allowed Helen to apply her make-up. But he didn't talk about it, did he? She wondered whether that was something Alekos would ever open up and discuss.

'You look stunning,' Helen enthused, standing back to admire the finished effect. 'Now, the dress.' She snapped her fingers and Nina passed it across. Slipping it deftly over Kelly's head, Helen straightened it and stood back, eyes narrowed. 'And now the shoes.'

Nina appeared again with something in her hand and Kelly pulled a face. 'I'll never be able to walk in those. I have a bit of a problem with shoes and shiny floors.'

'That's why God invented man. Alekos will hold your arm.' Helen placed them on the floor in front of her. 'They are perfect.'

As Kelly slid her feet into the shoes, Helen frowned at her. 'We just need to decide on jewellery—the neck is too bare.'

'Are you ready?' Alekos strode into the room with his phone to his ear, spectacularly handsome in a white dinner-jacket, an impatient frown touching his bronzed forehead as he clearly tried to conduct a conversation and finish dressing.

A black bow-tie hung round his neck ready to be tied and cufflinks gleamed at his wrists.

When he saw her, his conversation dried up and Kelly felt her heart beat faster.

She didn't need to look in the mirror to know that Helen had done her job well. Looking into his eyes was enough.

Impossibly excited about the celebration, and feeling incredible, Kelly turned and walked over to the mirror, treating him to a view of her bare back. The dress dipped low and she took his sudden indrawn breath to be a compliment. She needed that compliment because one glance in the mirror had told her that she looked nothing like herself. Normally she chose to wear black because it was safe. There was nothing safe about hot pink. It was bold and brave, but at the same time light-hearted and fun.

What bothered her most was that the dress was undeniably sexy.

And she wasn't sure it was a good idea to dress like this in front of Alekos.

They were supposed to be taking the whole sex element out of their relationship, weren't they?

On the other hand, if they were going to be celebrating what she thought they would be celebrating, then what better way to make their relationship complete?

'You look beautiful.' His voice husky, he dismissed the staff with a barely discernable movement of his head. 'I have something for you.'

Kelly's heart accelerated.

Staring up at him dreamily, she waited, wondering why he'd bought her another ring when she already had a beautiful one on her hand—the wrong hand, admittedly, but that could be easily rectified.

Alekos drew in a deep breath. 'But first there is something I want to say to you.'

Kelly smiled up at him mistily. 'There's something I want to say to you too.' *I love you. I've never stopped loving you.*

'I want to end this farce of sleeping in separate beds,' he breathed. 'It's driving me crazy. I can't concentrate on my work, I'm not getting any sleep.'

'Oh.' Slightly surprised by his approach, Kelly re-adjusted her expectations. It probably wasn't altogether surprising that he'd approached it from that angle, she reasoned. He was a healthy male with a powerful sex-drive. 'I feel the same way. It's driving me crazy, too.'

'I want a real relationship with you, and that includes sex.'

A real relationship.

'That's what I want too,' she whispered, her heart pounding as Alekos slid his hand behind her neck and pulled her mouth to his.

'I can't help myself.' He groaned the words against her lips. 'I have to just—'

'Oh yes.' The erotic slide of his tongue unleashed emotions that she thought she had well under control. After weeks of abstinence, Kelly went up in flames. She forgot that they were supposed to be going out. She even forgot that she was waiting for him to propose. Her body felt hot and tight, and everything inside her was focused on the moment.

Desperate for him, she gave a moan of encouragement as she felt his rough palms slide up her bare thighs. Her hand went to the button of his trousers and she felt the hard ridge of his arousal straining against her fingers.

His mouth was hot and demanding on hers, and Alekos bunched the silk dress as he shifted it out of the way impatiently. Kelly's arms locked around his neck and he lifted her where she stood, his dark eyes burning into hers as he gripped her hips.

'Kelly…'

'Yes, now,' she groaned. There was a brief pause and then he lowered her to the ground, his breathing a harsh rasp.

'Wait—we shouldn't.'

On fire and just desperate, Kelly clutched at the front of his dress shirt. 'Why?' She was breathless. 'I thought—'

'No.' His voice vibrating with tension, Alekos closed his hands over her arms and put her away from him. 'Not here. Not like this. That isn't what I meant.'

'No?'

'Later.' Smoothing her dress over her trembling body, Alekos took her face in his hands and kissed her. 'I don't want a few crazy minutes with you,' he said huskily. 'I want more than that.'

She wanted more than that too.

She wanted for ever, and when Alekos put his hand inside his jacket Kelly felt her heart stop.

'Alekos?'

'I have something for you.' His tone husky, Alekos withdrew a long, midnight-blue velvet box from his pocket. Kelly stared at it blankly, her brain refusing to compute the information that her eyes were transmitting. A long box: that was the wrong shape, wasn't it?

'What's that?' Her mind tried to explain away the anomaly. Maybe they'd run out of small boxes in the jewellers, or maybe he'd thought it would be more fun to disguise the gift as something different.

She was on the verge of telling him that he honestly hadn't needed to buy her another ring when he flipped open the box and watched her face in anticipation.

Kelly stared down at the glittering necklace, unable to pretend any longer.

'It's a necklace.'

Not a ring. A necklace.

'It will look perfect with your dress.' Alekos slid his fingers under the diamonds. 'I wanted to give you a present.'

He was giving her a present, Kelly thought wildly, not a future.

A necklace.

Not a ring.

Not a proposal.

Staring at the diamonds dangling from his fingers, Kelly felt the same way she'd felt when fallen flat on her face on the tiled floor. She was winded. Breathless. Slightly removed from reality.

Shocked and feeling quite ridiculously foolish, she didn't have a clue what to say, but she knew she had to say something because he was staring at her expectantly.

'I—' Nothing came out of her mouth. 'I don't know what to say.'

'You looked stunned.'

'Yes.' Her voice was flat; monotone. 'I am.'

'Diamonds do have that effect on people.'

Kelly forced herself to say something. 'It's very pretty. Thank you.' Her voice was stilted and polite, like a child thanking someone for a gift because a strict parent was looking at her expectantly.

Aware that Alekos was watching her with astonishment, Kelly realised that her response was probably less than appropriate, given the value of the gift, but she couldn't help it.

Somehow over the past few hours she'd managed to convince herself that he was going to propose—that the celebration that Helen had mentioned, was going to be their engagement.

Hot, embarrassing tears scalded her eyes. 'Thanks— it's lovely.'

'Then why are you crying?'

'I'm just—' She cleared her throat and tried to pull herself together. 'Well, a bit stunned. I wasn't expecting this.' Complete idiot that she was, she'd been expecting something different.

'I thought it could mark this new stage in our relationship.'

'The sex stage, you mean?'

'This necklace isn't about sex, Kelly.' Eyes narrowed, he watched her cautiously. 'Is that what you think?'

'No. No, I don't think that. I— Just ignore me. I'm pregnant, and pregnant women are often *emotional*.' She emphasised the word slightly, watching for signs of discomfort on his part, but he seemed perfectly calm. In fact, his only emotion was concern for her.

'Would you like to lie down? I wanted you to be there with me tonight, but if you're not well…'

He wanted her by his side, she reminded herself.

All right, so he hadn't proposed, but their relationship was going in the right direction. She was being horribly

unrealistic thinking that their relationship would be fixed in a few weeks. It was going to take much more than that, wasn't it?

She had to be patient.

Trying to calm herself down, Kelly pulled away from him and walked across to the mirror on legs so shaky it was as if she'd forgotten how to walk. He hadn't proposed, but things had changed between them. She could sense it.

For a start he'd called this house 'our' home, not 'my' home. And he had agreed to her suggestion that they leave sex out of the relationship, which showed that he was at least trying to accommodate her wishes. He saw her as his partner, not just a sex object. And, most importantly, when she'd said the word 'pregnant' he hadn't made a dash for his Ferrari.

That had to be a good sign.

CHAPTER SEVEN

SIMMERING with frustration across the table, Alekos watched with mixed feelings as Kelly charmed the group of high-powered businessmen. Bringing her with him had been a strategic move on his part to soften what would otherwise have been a difficult meeting. On the one hand he was relieved that the business side of things was going well, on the other he was raw with jealousy as he watched one of the younger men make her laugh.

It had been a long time since he'd seen Kelly so relaxed and happy.

She looked as though a light had been switched on inside her, as if she'd thrown off a weight of worry.

They were seated on the terrace of one of the best restaurants in Athens, shielded from other diners by a terrace of vines.

It was a perfect, blissful setting.

Alekos had never felt so on edge.

Not only was his temper reaching boiling point as he watched the young man flirt openly with Kelly, but his body still throbbed with sexual arousal because that one, torrid encounter in his villa had been nowhere near enough to satiate an appetite that had been building for far too long.

As Kelly leaned forward to reach for her water, the hot-pink dress gaped slightly and he saw a faint hint of shadow at the place where her breasts dipped. Sure that the other man was enjoying that view far more than the sights of Athens, Alekos tightened his fingers around his glass. He sat ultra-still, holding onto control by a thread.

Apparently oblivious to the danger he was facing, his business rival carried on his conversation. 'When Alekos said he was bringing a woman, we were not expecting someone like *you*.'

Listening to Kelly's delighted response to that outrageous flattery, Alekos tapped a slow and deadly rhythm on the table, his thoughts as black as thunder.

Was she doing it on purpose?

Was she trying to stoke his anger and jealousy?

'What do you think, Alekos?' It was Takis who spoke, the elder of the group of bankers. 'Will the expansion have a negative effect on profits?'

'I think,' Alekos purred as he watched the young man reach out to touch Kelly's golden hair, 'that if Theo does not take his hands off my woman within the next two seconds I will look elsewhere for finance.'

The man froze and his hand dropped to his lap.

Alekos smiled. 'Good decision.' He switched to Greek, knowing that Kelly wouldn't be able to follow the conversation. 'Touch her again and you will find yourself working at the supermarket checkout.'

Kelly was staring at him as if he'd gone mad.

Maybe he had, Alekos thought savagely, noticing that his knuckles on the glass were white. Never before had he lost control during what was, essentially, a business meeting. For once in his life he hadn't cared about the

end, only the means; if the means meant allowing some guy barely out of his cradle to paw Kelly, he wasn't interested.

Takis broke the sudden stillness around the table. He laughed and lifted his glass. 'Never underestimate what a Greek man will do when defending his woman, heh? We will drink to young love.' There was a faint ping as he tapped his glass against Alekos's. 'This relationship is serious, no?'

Alekos saw Kelly blush.

'It is time you settled down, that's good.' Takis gave a fatalistic shrug, as if it were a fate that befell every man eventually. 'You will need strong sons to take over that shipping business of yours. Kelly is not Greek, but—' he smiled forgivingly '—never mind. She is beautiful, and I can tell that she will give you strong sons.'

Alekos felt the familiar rush of blind panic. Sons: more than one. *Lots of children, all depending on him for their happiness and wellbeing.*

He reached for his wine glass and drank.

'The sooner you start, the better.' Takis didn't seem to notice the sudden crackle of tension and the stillness of Kelly's shoulders. 'The job of a Greek wife is to have Greek babies.'

Wondering whether Takis was tightening the screw on purpose, Alekos winced as he anticipated Kelly's outrage at that blatantly sexist comment. Intent on heading off bloodshed, he decided to intervene before she exploded. Their relationship, he thought, was too delicately balanced to weather too great a storm. 'This discussion is a little premature,' he said smoothly, but if he'd expected gratitude from Kelly he was disappointed.

She looked him in the eyes, her face as white as the napkin she placed carefully on the table in front of her.

'You think the discussion is premature? I think overdue would be a better word, don't you?'

Detecting something in her tone, Alekos lowered his glass slowly, aware of the sudden interest from everyone in the restaurant.

Her eyes suspiciously bright, Kelly stood up, her chair scraping on the floor. 'Excuse me,' she muttered stiffly. 'I need to use the bathroom.'

Exchanging looks of embarrassment and fascination, the men rose to their feet in a gesture of old-fashioned courtesy, and Alekos took one look at the ultra-shiny floor of the restaurant and decided that he'd better follow her.

He sprang upright, threw a final, fulminating look of warning towards the young businessman who was now several shades paler than he'd been at the beginning of the evening and followed Kelly.

The thin spike of her heel echoed on the marble, each angry tap a furious indicator of her mood. A few paces behind her, Alekos was treated to a close-up view of her incredible legs and wondered whether they could get away with leaving before dessert.

'You'd better take my arm before you slip,' he drawled as he lengthened his stride to catch up with her. 'And maybe you'd better not talk so much next time. I know Takis is old-fashioned when it comes to his views on women, but you almost blew that.'

'*I* blew it? You denied our baby!' She whirled to face him, her eyes furious and hurt. 'You're never going to change, are you? I'm just kidding myself. This past few weeks I thought you were coming round to the

whole idea, but the truth is that you'd just buried it. You're just doing what you do best—pretending it isn't happening!'

'That is not true.'

'It *is* true.' She virtually spat the words at him. 'When Takis said you should be thinking of babies, you said it was a little premature. Well, how much time do you need, Alekos?'

'I have no intention of discussing my private life with Takis Andropolous.'

'Oh, stop kidding yourself, Alekos! You don't want this baby. You never did. The only reason you're sticking with me is because you want sex. And don't you *dare* tell me that I was the one who almost blew the meeting—*you* were the one who sat there, all jealous and possessive, glaring at me across the table when I'm trying to chat to that guy *you* made me sit next to! You were the one who started a tirade of Greek, knowing I wouldn't be able to understand a word anyone was saying, and you were the one who left me sitting there drowning in all this testosterone and chest thumping while you lot were all glaring at each other!'

Alekos watched in appalled fascination as she drew breath. 'Kelly—'

'I haven't finished! I could have forgiven you for all that because you've obviously got some weird views on women that come with being Greek, but I will *never* forgive you for denying the existence of my baby.'

Swearing under his breath, Alekos shot a fulminating look at the riveted diners. 'I did *not* deny the existence of our baby.'

'You did! And don't you *dare* call it *our* baby. You haven't once mentioned it over the past few weeks. You buy me flowers, jewellery, anything you think might

soften me up so that I'll have sex with you, but do you think of the baby? No. Do you mention the baby? No. And *don't* use bad language in front of our child. I may not speak Greek, but I can tell from your tone of voice that you were saying something that no one under the age of eighteen should hear.'

In the interests of self-preservation Alekos decided that this probably wasn't a good time to point out that the baby wasn't even born yet. 'I wasn't softening you up so that I could have sex with you. If that was all I was interested in, then I would have just kissed you.'

'And that would have reduced me to rubble, is that what you're saying? Because you think you're such a sex god?' Her rage bubbled higher. 'You're arrogant, egotistical—'

'Kelly, you need to calm down.'

'Do *not* tell me to calm down!' She was literally shivering with emotion, her eyes bright and feverish in a face that was ghostly pale. 'This relationship ends now. This is not what I want for my child, and it isn't what I want for myself. I'm going home, and don't bother following me.' Her hands shaking, she tugged the ring off her finger and stuffed it into his hand. 'That's it. It's over. I want to go back to Corfu tonight because I can't bear to spend a single night under the same roof as you. Babies can sense things, you know. I'll fly back to England in the morning.' Barefoot, her head held high, she stalked towards the entrance of the restaurant without bothering to look over her shoulder.

Sodden with misery, Kelly lay alone in the middle of the huge bed in the villa in Corfu, drifting in that hazy place between sleep and wakefulness. Somewhere in the background there was a clacking sound which she

assumed to be the ceiling fan. She pulled the pillow over her head, feeling too low and exhausted to summon the energy to do anything about it.

By the time Alekos's pilot had flown her back to the island and the car had taken her back to the villa, it had been the middle of the night—not that it had made a difference, because she hadn't slept anyway.

Her eyes were sore with crying and there were too many thoughts bouncing around her head for her to have any hope of sleep.

The distinctive tread of male footsteps in her bedroom made her freeze with horror. Peeping from under the pillow, Kelly gave a horrified squeak.

Alekos stood there wearing the same dinner-jacket he'd worn the night before, only now the collar of his shirt was undone and the bow-tie was looped around his neck. His arms were loaded with packages and he stopped dead, apparently transfixed by the sight of her on the bed.

Still groggy, Kelly rubbed her eyes and tried to concentrate, but already her heart was racing, as it always did when he walked into a room. 'What are you doing here? And why are you still wearing your dinner-jacket? You look as though you've been up all night.'

'I have been up all night.' His dark eyes glittered with raw sexual appraisal and she remembered, belatedly, that she was naked.

'Stop staring at me.' Her face scarlet, she made a grab for the silk bed-cover, but she was lying on it and the process of extracting it turned into a writhing wrestling-match between her and the sheets that brought a sheen of sweat to Alekos's brow.

'Enough!' Depositing the parcels on the nearest chair, he strode across the room, yanked the bedcover free and threw it over her. '*Theé mou*, do you do this on purpose?'

'Do what on purpose?'

'Torment me.' He stepped back with his hands in the air as if touching her had scalded him; Kelly, awash with hormones and hideously overtired, exploded with emotion.

'Don't blame me! You're not even supposed to be here. I wanted to be on my own.' Too late, she realised that the clacking sound hadn't been the fan—it had been his helicopter landing.

'Tough.' Alekos shrugged off his jacket and threw it across the bottom of the bed. 'Our deal was that I was supposed to tell you what I'm thinking, so I came here to tell you what I'm thinking.'

'That was before, and—'

'Are you going to let me speak or do you want me to silence you in my favourite way?' His silky tone made her stiffen defensively and Kelly held the cover to her chin like a shield.

'I don't want you to touch me. Just say what you need to say and then go. I've booked myself on a flight at eleven o'clock.'

His eyes fixed on hers, Alekos drew in a deep breath. 'Last night at the restaurant you accused me of denying the existence of the baby. But that wasn't what I was doing.'

Kelly didn't give an inch. 'Well, it sounded like it from where I was sitting, and if you've come here to make excuses then you've wasted your time.'

'Kelly, you know I am a private man,' he said in a raw tone. 'I don't find it easy spilling my thoughts to

everyone, that isn't what I do. I am fully aware that our relationship is at an extremely delicate point—do you really think I was going to risk destabilising that by announcing your pregnancy to a bunch of strangers? Is that really what you wanted me to do?'

Too upset to consider a different point of view, Kelly sat stiff in the bed. 'You've been denying this baby ever since the moment I told you I was pregnant. I know you didn't want this. I know this is probably the worst thing in the world that could have happened to you, and pretending that isn't the case is just kidding yourself, Alekos. You're just hoping that the whole electric, sex-chemistry thing will somehow get us through this whole tangled mess.'

'That is *not* what I'm thinking. And it's true that finding out that you're pregnant has been difficult for me—I'm not denying that.' His voice was thickened, his accent more pronounced than usual. 'And I probably haven't coped with it as well as I should have done, but I *have* been trying. I readily agreed to your request that we sleep in separate rooms because part of me agreed with your reasoning.'

'Oh.'

'Yes, *oh*.' Visibly tense, he removed his cufflinks and rolled up the sleeves of his shirt. 'I admit that the sex between us does cloud judgement. I know I hurt you four years ago, but I am determined not to do it again, which is the other reason I agreed. I am trying to do as you asked and respect the boundaries you set for our relationship.'

'It's very unfair of you to suddenly start being so reasonable just because you know I'm angry,' Kelly muttered. 'And don't think for a moment that it changes any-

thing. Even if you're behaving like a reasonable person on the surface, I know you're still trying to pretend this whole baby thing isn't happening.'

He threw her a shimmering glance. 'I thought that the idea was that we focus on the relationship. You told me you didn't want to be with me just because of the baby—that it had to be right for us. I agreed. So I've been focusing on *us*. I bought gifts for you because I wanted to spoil *you*, but you interpret that as me ignoring the baby. If I'd bought gifts for the baby, you would have said that I was only trying to fix things because you were pregnant.'

Kelly swallowed and scraped her hair behind one ear. 'Maybe,' she said in a small voice. 'Possibly. Perhaps. Are you saying I'm unreasonable?'

'No.' He breathed out unsteadily. 'But I'm trying to point out that I can't win. Whatever I do can be misinterpreted if that's what you're determined to do. You don't trust me, and I don't blame you for that. In the circumstances it would be odd if you did. I know I have to earn your trust. I'm trying to do that.'

'You're turning this all around to make me feel bad. And none of that explains why you behaved like a caveman last night over dinner. You virtually thumped that guy! I know he was incredibly boring, but that's no excuse. I don't like violence.'

'And I don't like men trying to poach my woman.'

'You're very possessive.'

'I'm Greek.' Alekos gave a dangerous smile. 'And, yes, I'm possessive. That is one accusation I am not denying. Nor am I apologising. The day I smile on you flirting with another man is the day you know our rela-

tionship is dead. I will fight for our relationship, *agape mou*, even if that means offending your non-violent principles.'

Reluctantly fascinated by that unapologetically male, territorial display, Kelly found that her heart was pounding. 'I wasn't flirting with another man. I wasn't even enjoying his company,' she squeaked, a strange weakness spreading through her limbs as she eyed his pumped-up muscles and darkened jaw. 'If you want the honest truth, he was the most boring, creepy person I've ever sat next to.'

His eyes glittered dark and deadly. 'You were laughing and smiling. I've never seen you so happy.'

'You told me it was an important business meeting. I presumed you wanted me to be polite! And I was happy because, up until the point where you completely lost your mind, I really thought we were doing OK. You were being really nice to me; you called it *our* home, not *my* home, and I thought that meant we were making real progress, and—'

'Our home?' Alekos interrupted her, a curious look in his eyes, and Kelly gave a little shrug.

'That's what you called it: "our home". It made me feel all warm and fuzzy.'

'Warm and fuzzy? This is the same feeling you got from giving away a lump of money to a good cause, no?' Looking slightly dazed, Alekos jabbed his fingers into his hair and Kelly chewed one of her fingernails, wondering whether it was even possible for two people so different ever to understand each other.

'You made us sound like a pair,' she mumbled, trying to explain. 'A couple. We were an *us*. I honestly thought things were going really well, that's why I was happy. And when I'm happy I smile.'

His attention caught by that frank declaration, Alekos studied her intently. 'I presumed you were happy because of him.'

'I was happy because of *you*.' Kelly twisted the bedcover in her fingers. 'But don't get big-headed, because believe me it didn't last very long. You were completely vile during that dinner. And actually I feel pretty unappreciated, I can tell you, given that I worked so hard to be nice to him for your sake.'

'For my sake?'

'You told me it was an important meeting. I worked very hard to be nice to them and not let you down. And I was doing really well until you said that thing about the baby.' Remembering how she'd stalked out of the restaurant and left him to handle them on his own, Kelly covered her face with her hands, mortified. 'Now I feel bad. Which is horrible, because actually ninety percent of this was actually your fault.'

'I completely agree.'

Taken by surprise, Kelly peeped through her fingers. 'You agree?'

'Yes, I was monumentally insensitive. Until you pointed it out, it hadn't occurred to me how easy it would have been for you to misinterpret my reluctance to discuss the baby with strangers—but now I see that, yes, of course you were going to feel that way after I'd told you that I didn't want children.' Alekos yanked the bow-tie away from his neck and dropped it on top of the jacket. 'I have been up all night, trying to find ways of convincing you that I do want you and the baby.'

Distracted by the cluster of dark curls at the base of his throat, Kelly gulped. 'Up all night? Gosh, poor you, you must be so tired. Perhaps you'd better have a nap or something.'

'Sleep is not at the top of my list of priorities at the moment. Sorting this out is more important.' Alekos paced over to the chair where he'd deposited the parcels. 'I *do* think about the baby. Just to prove it to you, I thought it was time to deliver these: I've been buying them over the past few weeks, but I was afraid that if I gave them to you you'd take it the wrong way.' Filling his arms with the brightly wrapped boxes, he gave a rueful smile. 'It seems that by not giving them you took it the wrong way, so there doesn't seem any point in waiting.'

'What are they?' Kelly stared at the precarious tower of gifts in fascination. 'If that's jewellery, then you're going to need a bigger girlfriend.'

'It's not jewellery. None of this is for you. I bought gifts for the baby.'

Kelly blinked in amazement at the mountain of carefully wrapped presents. He'd bought gifts? For the baby? 'I—I'm not even two months' pregnant. We don't know what sex it is…'

'I did the wrong thing?' Alekos was as tense as a bow. 'I can take them back.'

'No. Don't do that.' He'd bought presents for the baby. Just when she'd thought he'd blocked it out of his mind, he'd been buying stuff.

'All right, now I feel really, *really* horrible,' Kelly confessed in a thick voice, and he gave a wry smile.

'I wasn't trying to make you feel horrible,' he said gruffly. 'I was trying to please you. That isn't proving as easy as I thought it would.'

'Thanks. That makes me feel even more horrible. What did you buy?'

'Open them and look.' Alekos gently spilled the parcels onto the bed and Kelly stared at the assortment of packages in disbelief.

'There are loads of them. I'm having one baby, not sextuplets.'

'I went shopping a couple of times when I flew to Athens.' Looking distinctly uncomfortable, he undid another button on his shirt. 'It's possible I may have got a little carried away.'

Touched that he'd thought about the baby during his hideously busy working day, and feeling more and more guilty that she'd misjudged him so badly, Kelly lifted the first parcel, which was large and extremely squashy. Ripping off the paper, she pulled out a huge brown bear sporting a red ribbon. 'Oh. It's *gorgeous*.'

'I thought if I bought one with a blue ribbon you'd be angry with me for assuming the baby was going to be a boy, and if I'd bought a pink ribbon and the baby was a boy then we would have had to change the ribbon…' His voice tailed off as he watched her face. 'So I thought red was best. Is it OK?'

Kelly, who had never before considered the purchase of a child's toy to involve a complex decision-making process—certainly not for a man who made decisions involving tens of millions of dollars every day—was stunned by the agonies he'd clearly endured in making his choice. 'It's really lovely. Perfect.' Noticing that the label said 'not suitable for children under eighteen months', she tucked it under the red ribbon so that he wouldn't see it, and made a mental note to position the bear in a strategic point in the nursery where the baby could see but not touch. 'I know the baby will love it.'

She opened the next parcel and found another bear, identical to the first. Bemused, but extra-careful not

to hurt his feelings, she smiled brightly. 'Another one. That's—great. Fantastic.' *What was he thinking? A bear for every day of the week?*

'You're thinking I've gone mad.'

'I'm not thinking that,' Kelly lied, and Alekos gently removed the bear from her grasp and stared down at it, a strange look in his eyes.

'My bear was the one constant in my life when I was little,' he said huskily. 'No matter how up and down my life, my bear was always there. I slept with him every night. And then one day I lost it. I took it to my grand-mother's, left it in the back of a taxi and never saw it again. I was devastated.' He lifted his head and gave her a mocking smile. 'Tell that to the press and you'll ruin my reputation for good.'

Hot tears scalded her eyes as she thought of the little boy losing his beloved bear. 'I—I'd never tell that to anyone,' she stammered, a lump in her throat. 'But couldn't you have got it back? Couldn't they have just phoned the taxi firm?'

'No one thought it was important enough.' Alekos handed the bear back to her carefully. 'I wanted our baby to have two identical bears, just in case. A spare is always useful. Maybe you can put one in a drawer or something. Then, if we have a crisis, we can sneak the other one into its place and avoid all that heartbreak.'

'OK, we'll do that.' The tears spilled down her cheeks, and Alekos looked at her in horror.

'Why are you crying? What have I done? Too many bears—not enough bears?'

'It isn't the bear,' she sobbed. 'I love the bears. Both of them. It's the fact that you had to go to sleep without it. I keep thinking about you, just six years old having to choose between your mum and dad, and it's just vile

and hideous; it's no wonder you're a bit screwed up about things.' Tears smeared her face and Alekos muttered something in Greek.

'You're crying over something that happened to me twenty-eight years ago?'

'Yes.' Kelly scrubbed her hand over her cheeks and tried to pull herself together. 'I think being pregnant might be making me a little bit emotional.'

'Very possibly,' Alekos said faintly, handing her a tissue. 'Just a little bit. I was worried I'd made a mistake with the bears.'

'The bears are beautiful.' She blew her nose hard. 'Both of them. And having a spare is a completely brilliant idea. I feel really bad now that I accused you of denying the baby when you'd already bought all that stuff. I want to make it up to you. I'm sorry I'm crying; I'm just so tired and I feel bad.'

'You have nothing to feel bad about,' he said softly, removing her tears with his thumb. 'I know I'm not good at this. And it's not surprising you're tired after last night. I upset you badly. I know I'm doing it all wrong, but I am trying, *agape mou*.'

'I know. What else have you bought?' It was an agonisingly tender moment and Kelly opened the other parcels one by one, touched by the variety of things he'd purchased. There were more toys, clothes in neutral colours and books in both Greek and English.

'I thought he ought to learn both languages.' Alekos watched her face as she unwrapped parcel after parcel. 'I want him to know that he is Greek.'

'*She.*' Kelly emphasised the word carefully as she stacked the books that undoubtedly wouldn't be read until the child was at least four. She grabbed another

tissue and blew her nose hard, not even wanting to think about how she must look. '*She* will also be half-English.'

'It is going to be a boy, I know it.'

'Even you can't dictate the sex of the child.' But Kelly was incredibly touched by the gifts. Most of them were completely inappropriate for a newborn, but it was the thought. 'They're all lovely, Alekos.'

'Good. So, now I have proved to you that I'm thinking of the baby, and you have explained to me that you weren't flirting, so everyone is happy.' Dragging his eyes away from her bare shoulders, Alekos sprang from the bed and strolled towards the bathroom. 'And now I'm going to take a long, cold shower because, while I agree with the theory of separate bedrooms, I am finding the reality rather hard to sustain. I'll meet you on the terrace for breakfast once I have given myself frostbite.'

CHAPTER EIGHT

KELLY stood with her hand on the door to the bathroom, listening to the sound of water running.

Raising her eyes to the ceiling, she gave herself a lecture. *What was wrong with her?* Whether they had sex or not wasn't going to have an adverse effect on how this relationship progressed. In fact, she was fast coming to the conclusion that the opposite was true: abstaining made it hard to think about anything *but* sex. It was like giving up chocolate: the moment you knew you couldn't have it, it became impossible to think of anything else.

Kelly opened the door before she could change her mind.

Alekos stood under the shower with his eyes closed, the stream of water running off his broad shoulders onto his washboard-flat abdomen and down his hard thighs.

Kelly gulped and quickly lifted her eyes, but that didn't help much because then she just found herself looking at the perfect symmetry of his handsome face and the sensual lines of his mouth.

Dropping her robe on the floor, she moved silently across the bathroom, walked under the stream of water and slid her arms around his waist.

'I wondered how long you were going to stand there just looking,' he drawled, and Kelly glanced up at him.

'You had your eyes shut. How did you know I was standing there?'

'I can sense you.' His eyes opened and he gave a slow, dangerous smile. 'That, and I heard the door open. Unless my housekeeper has suddenly developed a desire to see me naked, it had to be you.'

Kelly was fairly sure that every one of his female household-staff harboured a desire to see him naked, but she tried to block out that fact.

She gasped as water trickled over her shoulder. 'You weren't kidding about the cold shower. This water is *freezing.*'

'You can take that as a compliment.'

Shivering, her teeth chattering and her flesh covered in goose bumps, Kelly giggled. 'Is it really that bad?'

His answer was to guide her hand to the bold swell of his erection. 'Bear in mind that this is with the aid of *really* cold water.'

Kelly closed her hand over him and heard the breath hiss through his teeth. 'I'd say the cold water isn't working. Maybe we need to try something else.' Turning off the flow of water with her hand, she dropped to her knees and took him in her mouth.

She didn't need to understand Greek to pick up the shock in his tone, shock that quickly turned to a groan of pleasure as her mouth caressed the whole thick, velvet length of him. He was hot and hard, and she heard the harsh rasp of his breathing as she used her lips and tongue, driving him wild.

'Kelly…' His voice raw, he lifted her to her feet and looked down at her, his eyes narrow slits of burning desire. 'You never did that before.'

'That was before—this is now.' The heat of his erection brushed against her belly and as his hungry mouth caught hers in a hot, sexy kiss a shudder ran through her.

She wanted to tell him how she was feeling, but the words wouldn't string themselves together into a coherent sentence.

Alekos pressed her back against the wall of the shower and Kelly gasped as his hand slid between her thighs. She was trying to work out how to breathe and say his name at the same time when his fingers slipped skilfully inside her. As he touched in all the right places, sensation pooled in her pelvis and her eyes drifted shut.

She was on fire, every single part of her was on fire, and she tried to tell Alekos that he needed to turn the cold water on again, but his mouth was devouring hers and she couldn't catch her breath to speak.

She wanted to tell him that she felt incredible—that he was incredible—but before she could speak, he scooped her up in his arms and carried her through to the bedroom.

'I'm still wet,' Kelly mumbled dizzily and he gave a slow, dangerous smile.

'I know you are, *agape mou*.' Gently pushing her legs apart, he slid down her body, proving his point.

Aware of the hot scorch of the late-morning sun shining directly through the open doors, Kelly squirmed in embarrassment, but he ignored her attempts to close her legs, clamping her wrists together with one hand and using the other to do exactly as he wanted.

With each caress, each skilful, intimate stroke of his tongue, he brought her closer and closer to orgasm. As Kelly wriggled and squirmed in an attempt to relieve the burning sensation in her pelvis, Alekos pinned her hips with his hands, subjecting her to something close to sensual torture.

His tongue was slick and clever, his fingers skilled and knowing, and Kelly felt heat spread through her like a flash fire. Her climax hit with the shattering force, the pleasure pushing her higher and higher as she cried out his name and dug her nails into the smooth muscle of his shoulders. Her pleasure went on and on and he experienced every moment of it with her, his fingers buried deep inside her, his mouth tasting her pleasure.

While she was still shaking in the aftermath, Alekos slid up her body, pushed her thighs still wider and entered her with a smooth, purposeful thrust that joined them completely. Kelly cried out his name as white-hot lightning shot through her, searing her body with sensations so overwhelming that she couldn't breathe.

He made a rough sound deep in his throat and then his mouth came down on hers, the erotic demands of his kiss sending the excitement spinning higher and higher. Cupping her bottom in his hand, Alekos lifted her and thrust deep, the slow, sensual movement of his hips creating almost unbearable pressure as he filled her.

Kelly locked her arms around his neck, and when he lifted his head and looked into her eyes the connection between them deepened to something so incredibly personal that she felt something unravel inside her.

Alekos slid his hand over her thigh, encouraging her to curl her leg across his back. Kelly did as he urged, feeling the sensations intensify as he drove deep, each skilled thrust propelling them both towards climax. The

heat was unbearable; her nerve endings were sizzling and when the explosion finally came it took both of them down together. The power of it shocked her and she dug her nails into his shoulders again, her heart pounding, her body slick against his as he drove into her for a final time.

Breathless, stunned, she lay there listening to his harsh breathing, feeling the tension in his slick shoulders. And then he gathered her against him and hugged her tightly. 'Tell me I wasn't too rough.'

Feeling too weak to speak, all Kelly could manage was a brief shake of her head, and Alekos frowned as he pushed her tangled hair away from her face with a gentle hand.

'I was too rough?'

'You were perfect,' she croaked and he gave a slow, satisfied smile as he rolled onto his back, holding her against him.

'I was trying to be extra-gentle,' he murmured, kissing the top of her head. 'But you're so much smaller than me.'

Pressed against the hard muscle of his shoulder, Kelly was well aware of that fact. 'You're—it was—'

'Incredible.' His grip on her tightened. '*You* were incredible. Especially given the amount of light in the room.'

Kelly's face burned at the memory of his intimate exploration. 'You didn't exactly give me a choice.'

'After your performance in the shower, *erota mou*, it is a waste of time pretending to me that you are a shrinking virgin.' A sardonic gleam in his eye, Alekos ran his tongue over the seam of his mouth suggestively, and Kelly wondered how it was that she could still feel completely desperate for him.

'Maybe you do need a bit more practice.' She slid her hand slowly down his body, entranced by the differences between them. Her thigh was pale against the bronzed, hair-roughened length of his, soft against hard and strong, feminine against masculine.

'Keep doing that and we won't be getting up today.' Alekos gave a slow smile and closed his hands over her hips, shifting her so that she straddled him.

Feeling him pressed hard against her, Kelly gave a soft gasp. 'What are you doing?'

'I happen to like the view from here,' he said huskily, his jaw clenching as Kelly took the initiative and slowly slid herself onto his erection.

From this angle she was able to watch his face and she felt a flash of satisfaction as his eyes darkened. Slowly rotating her hips, she took him deeper, and this time she was the one who shackled his hands, pinning them above his head as she rode him.

It gave her a sense of power, holding him there, even though she knew he could free himself in a minute and take control.

Leaning forward, she licked at his mouth, smiling against his lips as she felt his strong fingers biting into her hips.

'*Theé mou*, you feel incredible,' he groaned, meeting each swirl of her hips with his own rhythmic thrusts. Kelly's hair fell forward, forming a curtain as they kissed, their bodies moving together as everything grew sharper and hotter.

She felt him tense beneath her, felt his grip on her hips tighten, and then his final thrust hurled them both forwards into an explosion of sensation. The intensity

of her orgasm shattered her and she pressed her mouth to the sleek skin of his shoulder, sobbing his name as they tumbled over the edge together.

'Why four children?' His mobile in his hand, Alekos leaned across and adjusted the angle of Kelly's hat, making sure that her skin was protected from the burning heat of the sun.

'It just seems like a nice number. I was an only child. I always thought childhood was probably easier if there were more of you. A sister would have been great, someone to laugh, cry and paint your toenails with. How about you?'

'I've never felt much of a need for someone to paint my toenails with.'

Kelly grinned and emptied another blob of sunscreen onto her leg. 'I'm quite relieved about that, actually.'

'Do you want me to rub that in for you?'

'No.' Blushing, she smoothed the cream over her leg. 'Last time you did that, we ended up back in bed.'

A slight smile touched the corner of his mouth and he watched her with lazy amusement. 'And that's a problem?'

'No.' Not a problem at all. *He made her feel beautiful.* 'But I'm enjoying talking to you.'

'I can talk and perform at the same time,' he said silkily, and Kelly shot him a warning look, trying to ignore the immediate response of her heart.

'Try and last six seconds without thinking about sex. Try really hard.'

'If you're going to flaunt yourself in a miniscule bikini, then you are asking the impossible.'

'You bought me the bikini.' But she loved the fact that he couldn't get enough of her. 'I don't suppose I'll

be fitting into this for much longer anyway.' From under the brim of her hat, Kelly sneaked a glance at him, testing the temperature of his mood, wondering if the reference to her pregnancy would upset the balance of the atmosphere.

Alekos was frowning down at his mobile. 'Excuse me. I need to make a call.' He sprang to his feet and paced to the far end of the terrace, his shorts riding low on his lean hips, his feet bare.

Unable to decide whether his sudden need to make a phone call was the result of her mentioning the baby, Kelly felt a flash of anxiety. Even after ten days of almost continuous love-making she still couldn't completely relax. Electrifying sex and generous gifts hadn't been enough to delete the dull ache of worry that gnawed away at the pit of her stomach. And her anxiety was not without foundation, was it? Alekos had made no secret of the fact he hadn't wanted children. Even if she now understood and was sympathetic to the reason, it didn't change the fact that this wasn't what he would have chosen.

A person didn't change overnight, did they?

She'd grown up watching her mother try to convert her father from wild boy to family man. It hadn't worked.

Watching Alekos, Kelly felt a flicker of unease, unable to dismiss the fact that he'd made the call after she'd brought up the subject of the baby. Was he using it as an escape from a subject he found hard to discuss? Did it mean he was still having trouble accepting the situation?

She watched him as he paced the terrace and talked, gesturing with his hands, making an instantaneous shift from Mediterranean lover to ruthless businessman while she reasoned with herself.

He was here, wasn't he? That had to count for something—a lot, actually. Of course he wasn't going to get used to the idea overnight, but he was obviously trying.

Attempting to push away the dark mist that was pressing at the edges of her happiness, Kelly glanced round the beautiful gardens that tumbled from the sunlit terrace down to the beach. The rioting, colourful Mediterranean plants attracted birds and bees, and the only sound in the air was the cheerful chirrup of the cicadas and the occasional faint splash as a swallow swooped to steal water from the swimming pool.

It was paradise.

Paradise with a cloud on the horizon.

Ending the phone call, Alekos strode back to her, simmering with frustration. 'What do you do when two of the children in your class constantly scrap?'

'I separate them,' Kelly said instantly and he looked at her, eyes narrowed.

'You separate them?'

'Yes. I don't let them sit together. If they sit together then they focus on their interaction rather than their work. They put all their energies into being in conflict with the person next to them, rather than listening to me.'

'Genius,' Alekos breathed, dialling another number and lifting the phone to his ear. He spoke in Greek, his tone clipped and businesslike as he delivered what sounded like a volley of instructions.

Kelly waited patiently until he'd finished talking. 'What was that all about?'

'Two of my very senior executives seem unable to interact without generating major conflict.' Alekos strolled to the small table and poured some lemonade for her. 'They're both too good to lose, and I've been trying to find a way of making them work together. It hadn't occurred to me to separate them. It's a brilliant idea.'

Kelly flushed with pleasure, ridiculously pleased by his praise, and incredibly relieved that it obviously was a really pressing crisis that had driven him to take that call, nothing to do with the baby. 'So that's what you've done?'

'Yes.' Ice cubes clinked as they tumbled into the glass. 'I've moved one of them to Investor Relations. Perfect. I think you should come and work for my company. You can sort out all the people problems that drive me demented. You're very clever.' He handed her the drink and she took it gratefully, touched again by his praise.

'I'm just a schoolteacher,' she muttered. 'I teach eight-year-olds.'

'Which makes you extremely well qualified to deal with my board,' Alekos drawled, glancing at his watch. 'Go and get dressed into something slightly less provocative. I want to take you out.'

'Out?'

'Yes. If you want to talk and not have sex then we'd better go somewhere extremely public.'

He took her to Corfu town and they wandered hand in hand around the old fortress, mingling with the tourists. 'Did you always want to be a teacher?'

'Yes.' Kelly was rummaging in her bag. 'When I was small I used to line my toys up in a row and give them lessons. Alekos, I've lost my sunglasses and my new iPod. I *know* I put them in my bag. I think.'

'Your sunglasses are on your head. I have your iPod.' Visibly amused, Alekos pulled it out of his pocket and handed it to her. 'You left it in the kitchen. Maria found it.'

'The kitchen?' Kelly took it from him gratefully, trying to remember when she'd taken it to the kitchen. 'How weird.'

'It was in the fridge,' he said dryly, and she gave a helpless shrug.

'Even more weird. I suppose I must have left it there when I was pouring myself a glass of milk.'

'That sounds completely logical.' His voice was gently mocking. 'If I lose any of my possessions, the first place I look is the fridge.'

'You never lose anything because you're scarily organised. You ought to loosen up a bit. And it's mean to tease me. I'm just really tired.' Her comment wiped the indulgent smile from Alekos's face.

'We will go home and I will call the doctor.'

'I don't want to go home and I don't need a doctor,' Kelly said mildly, pushing her iPod deep into her bag to avoid losing it again. 'I'm pregnant, not ill.' Glancing at him, she noticed the sudden tension in his shoulders and sighed. It was like waiting for a bomb to go off. 'I just need a decent night's sleep.' And she needed to stop lying there worrying that he was going to change his mind and walk out any day. 'It doesn't help that you're insatiable.'

'I seem to recall *you* were the one who woke *me* at five this morning.'

Kelly turned scarlet as two women turned their heads to stare. 'Could you keep your voice down?'

'They shouldn't be listening to a private conversation.'

But Kelly knew that the truth was that wherever they went women stared. Alekos attracted female attention. Slightly uneasy about that fact, she changed the subject. 'I expect you did well at school. You're very clever.'

'I was bored stiff.'

Kelly gave a strangled laugh. 'I pity your poor teachers. I wouldn't have wanted to teach you.'

Alekos stopped and pulled her into his arms, smoothing her hair away from her face with his hand. 'You *are* teaching me,' he said huskily. 'All the time. Every day I learn something new from you. How to be patient. How to solve a problem in a non-violent way. How to find an iPod in a fridge.'

'Ha ha, very funny.' Her heart was thundering like horses' hooves in a race, because he was so indecently good-looking and all his attention was focused on her. 'You're teaching me stuff, too.'

He gave a slow, dangerous smile. 'Perhaps you'd better not list exactly what I'm teaching you while we're in a public place. That's why we came here, remember?'

'I didn't mean *that*.' A warm, fluttery feeling settled low in her belly, a feeling that increased as he lowered his mouth to kiss her.

Alekos led her along a narrow back-street and into a tiny restaurant where he was greeted like a hero.

'My grandmother used to bring me here. It is traditional Corfiot cooking.' Alekos pulled out a chair for her. 'You will enjoy it.'

'You adored your grandmother.' Kelly twisted the ring on her finger self-consciously. 'I feel so guilty that

I almost sold this. I had no idea it was hers. And I didn't have a clue that it was that valuable. I almost had a heart attack when I saw that bid.'

'But not as big a heart attack as when you saw me standing at the school gates and realised that I'd bought it.'

'That's true.' Kelly wanted to ask whether he'd intended to give it to Marianna, but she decided that their fragile relationship didn't need any more external bombardment. 'It was a shock.'

'Why did you choose to teach in that place? You could have taught in a big school in a city.'

Kelly watched in surprise as several waiters arrived carrying a dozen small plates of different Greek specialities. 'When did we order? Or did they just read your mind?'

'They give you whatever the kitchen has freshly prepared. If you want authentic Greek cooking, then this is the place to come. You haven't answered my question.'

'About why I chose Little Molting? I wanted to keep a low profile.'

In the process of spooning *dolmades* onto her plate, Alekos paused. 'A low profile?'

Kelly picked up her fork, wondering how honest to be. 'The whole press thing was a bit overwhelming after our wedding that didn't happen. They wouldn't leave me alone. Only because I was linked to you, of course,' she said hastily, her hair falling forward as she studied the food on her plate. 'Not because I'm interesting by myself. And, actually, I wouldn't really want all that. Can you imagine what they'd print about me in one of those celebrity magazines? "And Kelly has graciously invited us to photograph her in her beautiful home. And

here we are in her kitchen where you see that, oh dear, she has forgotten to empty the bins".' Realising that Alekos hadn't said a word, her voice tailed off and she looked up at him. 'What? I'm talking too much?'

'The doctor said that the press hounded you on our wedding day.'

Kelly tucked her hair behind her ear. 'Yes, well, you not turning up at the wedding was quite exciting for them, I suppose. For reasons I've never understood, some people thrive on the misery of others. Watching someone coping with trauma appears to be a popular spectator-sport. I don't get it myself. If I see someone upset I either want to comfort them or give them privacy, not ogle them, but there you are—people are sometimes a bit disappointing, aren't they?'

'*Theé mou*, I am truly sorry for what I put you through.' His voice was hoarse and he reached across the table and caught her hand. 'I didn't think about the press or the attention that would be focused on you.'

'That's because you live your life behind high walls and you have security men who make the Incredible Hulk look puny.' Kelly stared down at the strong, bronzed fingers covering hers. She wondered if he realised that she was still wearing his ring on her right hand. Maybe he'd just forgotten; men were pretty rubbish at noticing things like that, weren't they? She tapped her fingers on the table, hoping to draw attention to it. 'Are you right-handed or left-handed?'

Alekos looked astonished by the sudden change of subject. 'Right-handed. Why?'

Because I'm trying to bring up the subject of hands, Kelly thought wildly, deciding that subtlety wasn't her

strong point. 'I'm right-handed too.' She waggled her hand, making sure that the diamond flashed in his face.

'You're right-handed.' He looked at her cautiously. 'I suppose it's always useful to know these things. I really am sorry that you were subjected to so much press attention.'

Nowhere near as sorry as she was that he hadn't said anything about her wearing his ring on her right hand. Kelly put her hand back in her lap, despondent. 'It's OK—well, not completely OK, of course. I *was* very upset. It was jolly humiliating, if I'm honest. I was pretty angry with you.'

'*Pretty* angry? You should have been livid.'

'All right, I was livid,' she confessed. 'I felt like a total idiot ever thinking that someone like you could be interested in someone like me.' Maybe she was still behaving like an idiot. Maybe it was idiotic to think that this could ever work. 'Billionaires don't usually hang around with penniless students. Not in the real world.'

'Then they ought to,' Alekos drawled. 'They might be happier.'

Kelly looked at him, wanting to ask if he was happy—*wanting to ask how he was feeling about the baby now that several weeks had passed*. But broaching that subject felt like handling a priceless Ming vase: she was too afraid she might smash the whole thing to pieces if she touched it in the first place.

'If it would help, you can hit me now.' Alekos studied her across the table, clearly sensing the undercurrents but mistakenly attributing them to the past rather than the present. 'You might find it cathartic.'

'I'm non-violent,' Kelly muttered. 'I don't think it would have made me feel any better to bruise your face, then or now.'

'It might make *me* feel better.'

She looked up at him, slightly reassured by the fact that he clearly regretted the way he'd treated her. At least he hadn't *tried* to hurt her.

'I understand better now.' She pushed her fork into piece of spicy local sausage. 'Things were really intense between us. We barely stopped kissing long enough to have a conversation. Neither of us really thought further than the moment. And I was all over you, saying stuff because I'm useless at holding it all in. I've thought about what you said—about waking up that morning and seeing the story in the magazine about me wanting children. It's no wonder you freaked out.'

Alekos drew in a deep breath. 'You don't have to make excuses for me.'

'I'm not. I'm just saying that I can understand it better now. Maybe if that magazine had come out the day before, or even the day after, we could have talked about it, and who knows?' Kelly shrugged. 'The morning of the wedding was just basically very bad timing.'

'What I did to you was unforgiveable.'

'It wasn't unforgiveable. It was hurtful, scary—loads of things, actually.' Thinking back to that time made her feel slightly sick. 'But it wasn't unforgiveable. Especially not now I understand why you reacted that way. I shared some of the blame for just diving into a hot, intense relationship with you without discussing the really important things.'

Alekos studied her for a long moment. 'You are the most generous person I have ever met,' he said gruffly, and Kelly blushed.

'Not that generous. I said a few bad things to Vivien about you, I can promise you that.' Agonisingly conscious of him, she looked down at her plate. 'Do you forgive me for selling your ring?'

'Yes.' He replied without hesitation. 'I drove you to that.'

'If it belonged to your family, why did you let me keep it in the first place?'

'It was a gift to you.'

'Well, that was a very generous gift. I had no idea it was worth—' she lowered her voice to a whisper '—four-million dollars.'

'It is worth a great deal more than that,' Alekos said calmly. 'Try this lamb. It's cooked in herbs and it's delicious.'

'More?' Kelly's voice was a squeak and Alekos smiled.

'The ring has been passed down my father's side of the family for generations.' He toyed with the stem of his glass. 'My great-great-great-grandfather was apparently given it as a reward for saving the life of an Indian princess. Or so the legend goes.' A cynical smile touched his mouth. 'I suspect the stone may have less romantic origins, but I've never explored it further.'

'I don't even want to know how much it's worth,' Kelly said faintly, glancing cautiously over her shoulder to check the other diners weren't listening. 'As soon as we leave this place, I'm giving it back to you. It's crazy giving anything that valuable to me! I'll leave it in the fridge or something. You know I'm useless.'

'It is perfectly safe on your finger.' Amused, Alekos dismissed her concerns, but Kelly stared down at the

sparkling, winking diamond, no longer to able to pretend that he might have forgotten she was wearing it on the finger of her right hand.

He hadn't forgotten.

So why hadn't he suggested she move it to her left hand?

On the surface they appeared to be getting on well, but he still hadn't talked about the future, had he? He hadn't mentioned marriage.

He hadn't said 'I love you'.

And neither had she, because this time she was terrified of saying the wrong thing. Of spilling out something he didn't want to hear. Every time they made love she had to clamp her mouth shut, terrified that the words might fly out by themselves in an unguarded moment of ecstasy.

Her appetite gone, Kelly put her fork down and took a sip of water.

It was early days, she told herself firmly. It was going to take time to rebuild what they had. And, anyway, they were building something new. Something better. Something deeper and more enduring.

That wasn't something that could be rushed. He was right to wait. She had to give it time.

But telling herself that did nothing to alleviate the sick feeling in the pit of her stomach.

CHAPTER NINE

'WE'RE flying to Italy for one evening?' Kelly decided that she'd never be able to be as cool as he was about foreign travel. 'Where, exactly?'

'Venice. We're attending a reception at a gallery.' Alekos didn't quite meet her eyes and she had a distinct feeling that there was something he wasn't telling her.

'And they like you because you're rich and you spend money? Can we go on a gondola?' She was talking to his shoulders because he'd already walked into his dressing room.

'That's for tourists.'

'*I'm* a tourist.' Bouncing off the bed, Kelly followed him into the dressing room. 'I've always wanted to go on a gondola.'

Selecting a suit and a fresh white shirt, Alekos gave a tense smile. 'All right. I'll take you on a gondola to-morrow before we come home. Tonight is a very smart gathering. You need to dress up.'

Kelly rested her hand over her stomach self-consciously. 'I'll have to wear something baggy; my tummy is sticking out. It must be too much Greek food.'

'Or it could be our baby,' Alekos said softly, placing his hand over hers. For a moment his eyes lingered on

hers and then he lowered his head and kissed her on the mouth. 'I bought you a dress.' Reaching into the wardrobe, he retrieved a large box decorated with a subtle, tasteful logo. 'I hope you like it.'

'You mean you hope it covers my fat tummy. At least I have an excuse—the worst thing is when someone asks you when the baby is coming and you have to tell them you're not pregnant.' Light-headed, thrilled by his unexpected warmth towards the baby, Kelly chatted away. 'It's almost worth being pregnant for ever just so that you have an excuse when your clothes are too tight. Oh.' She removed the dress from the tissue paper and stared at it in awe. 'It's stunning. Gold. Long.'

'Is it all right?'

Kelly wondered why he was asking her that when he'd bought her clothes before without ever asking her opinion. Why be worried about this one? Unless it really was a very important evening. 'The dress is perfect.'

'I hope you don't trip over the hem.'

'Me too. With any luck there won't be any stairs,' she said hopefully, fingering the fabric with deference. 'Where did you buy it?'

Alekos turned away from her and delved inside the pocket of his suit, searching for something. 'It was made especially by an Athenian designer,' he said vaguely. 'I gave her your measurements.'

Was it her imagination or was he suddenly a little tenser than he'd been a few moments before? Picking up an atmosphere but not understanding it, Kelly was worried she hadn't been enthusiastic enough. Perhaps he thought she was being ungrateful.

'I love it. Honestly, it's gorgeous. I've never had anything made especially for me before.' She delved in the box and pulled out a pair of shoes made from the same fabric. Eyeing the heels, she gave a faltering smile. 'Will there be a lot of valuable items on display for me to crash into?'

'You won't be crashing anywhere tonight, *agape mou*.' Relaxed again, Alekos strolled towards the shower. 'Your stylist will be here in half an hour, so why don't you grab some rest while you can?'

'My stylist.' Kelly grinned to herself. 'I'm not sure why that sounds so good. I ought to be able to style myself, but it's awfully nice to know that there will be someone else to blame if you end up looking a total mess. Are we coming home tonight?'

'No. We're booked into a suite at the Cipriani.'

'The Cipriani? I've heard of that,' Kelly squeaked. 'Wow. Lots of famous people stay there: George Clooney, Tom Cruise, Alekos Zagorakis…'

'And Kelly,' Alekos finished, and she gave a weak smile.

'And Kelly. I just hope George Clooney doesn't feel upstaged by me being there. Poor him. He doesn't stand a chance, does he?'

As the limousine pulled up to the end of a long red carpet, Kelly shrank. 'You didn't say anything about a red carpet, cameras and a million people staring. Alekos, I can't walk in these shoes in public.'

'If I'd mentioned it, you just would have worried.' Alekos took her hand and gave it a squeeze. 'I'm with you this time. You just smile and look aloof.'

'It's hard to look aloof when you're nose is splattered on the floor, which is where mine will be if I have to walk the length of that carpet in front of an audience!'

'I'll be holding your hand.'

'Can I take my shoes off?'

'Not unless you want to attract extra attention. Smile,' Alekos instructed as the car door was opened from the outside and a burst of light filled the car. 'Leave the rest to me.'

Kelly stepped gingerly out of the car and was immediately blinded by flashbulbs. Her lips fixed in a rigid smile, she took one look at the yelling crowd, and would have shot back into the car but Alekos's fingers handcuffed her wrists.

'Walk. Incline your head. Lift your chin slightly— better.' He issued a stream of instructions and encouragement, his hand holding hers tightly as he walked her down the red carpet and into the gallery. 'Now you can relax.'

'Are you kidding?' Kelly stared nervously at the priceless artefacts. 'I won't relax until I leave knowing I didn't break anything.'

'If you do break something, no one will dare comment,' Alekos said smoothly. 'I'm an extremely generous benefactor. And, no, before you ask, that doesn't give me warm, fuzzy feelings.'

'I don't think even I'd get warm, fuzzy feelings about a painting,' Kelly confessed, craning her neck as she looked at the art on the walls. 'Why do you support a museum in Venice? Why not the museum in Athens?'

'I do support the museum in Athens. Come with me, there is someone I want you to meet.' Supplying her with a drink, Alekos led her through the elegant throng of people towards a man who stood admiring a painting. 'Constantine.'

The man turned and Kelly saw that he was elderly. His white hair was swept back from a face that was still handsome, despite his years. 'Alekos.' His expression brightened and there was a brief exchange of rapid Greek before Alekos drew Kelly forward and introduced her.

'Ah.' Constantine smiled at her, a knowing look in his eyes. 'So we are surrounded by priceless works of art but still Alekos manages to arrive with something more dazzling on his arm.' He lifted her hand to his lips. 'Even the gold of the Renaissance doesn't shine quite so brightly as a woman in love. Good, I'm pleased. And not before time, Alekos Zagorakis.'

Kelly felt Alekos stiffen beside her and suddenly she wanted to put her hand over the other man's mouth to silence him.

She'd been walking on eggshells for weeks, and now this man was stomping over their fragile relationship with hobnail boots.

'I love this painting,' she blurted out in a high voice. 'Is it a—?' Suddenly her brain emptied; she couldn't think of a single Italian artist. Panic had wiped her mind clean. 'Canaletto?'

Constantine looked at her curiously and then shifted his gaze to the information plate next to the painting that clearly said *Bellini*.

Kelly gave a weak smile. 'Bellini—of course. I wonder if they have any postcards that I can buy for the children…' Gabbling nervously, it took her a moment to realise she'd inadvertently said totally the wrong thing.

'Children? You have children?' Constantine glanced from her to Alekos who was standing as frozen as a statue. 'This is good news. Is there a reason for me to congratulate you?'

Horrified, Kelly sneaked a look at Alekos, whose face was a study in masculine tension.

'No,' he said shortly. 'You have no reason to congratulate me.'

'I meant the children that I teach. I'm a teacher.' But Kelly's legs were shaking and she put her hand against the wall to support herself.

Constantine slapped Alekos on the shoulder. 'So you're not a father yet?'

'No.' Alekos's voice was hoarse. 'I'm not a father.'

Kelly felt as though he'd punched her.

She felt hideously, horribly sick. Had he really said that?

He still wasn't telling anyone. He was still denying the existence of the baby.

Not trusting herself to speak, Kelly wished she could drink the champagne that was circulating, but she had to settle for orange juice which proved absolutely useless for numbing pain. Alekos had smoothly changed the subject, but Kelly was so upset she couldn't even bring herself to look at him. Her hands shook so much,

she sloshed orange onto the floor. Normally she would have been mortified by her clumsiness, but tonight she didn't even care.

I'm not a father. He'd actually said those words.

I'm not a father.

What was she doing with him? She was a complete and utter fool, trying to shape this relationship into something that looked normal.

She was kidding herself if she ever thought he was going to suddenly come round to having children. And just because she was sympathetic to his reasons didn't mean she was willing to allow her child to have the same dysfunctional relationship with him that she'd had with her father. No way was she going to have her child waiting on a doorstep for a father who just wasn't interested.

I'm not a father.

'Alekos!' A woman with sloe eyes and an impossibly slender frame joined their group, kissing first Alekos and then Constantine. 'Isn't this a terrible crush? Still, it's good to do one's bit for the arts.' Her eyes fastened on Kelly's dress and then widened. 'Is that—?'

'Tatiana, this is Kelly.' Alekos interrupted the woman swiftly but Kelly stared at her numbly, wondering why her dress was causing such a stir.

Why was everyone so shallow? Yes it was pretty, and she liked having something special to wear as much as the next girl, but no dress, however gorgeous, could make up for a completely deficient relationship.

I'm not a father.

'Why are you staring at my dress?'

Tatiana laughed, a sound like glass shattering. 'It's by Marianna, isn't it? Lucky you. She only designs for the favoured few. Completely impossible to get hold of any of her pieces.' She gave Alekos a knowing smile. 'Unless you have a particular place in her heart, of course.'

By Marianna.

Marianna?

Kelly stared at the woman. Then she looked down at the gold dress, remembering how tense Alekos had been when he'd given it to her.

No wonder, she thought numbly. No wonder he'd been behaving oddly.

He must have been terrified that she'd find out.

What sort of insensitive brute dressed his current girlfriend in his ex's creations?

The same insensitive brute who still denied the existence of their baby. The same insensitive brute who hadn't told her to move her ring to the other hand.

Her eyes scalded by tears, Kelly stared hard at the Bellini on the wall, wondering if Renaissance man had been any more considerate than modern man.

Fisting her hand into the gold dress, she pulled it off the ground and swept towards the exit, brushing against a fine Renaissance sculpture in her attempt to get away as fast as possible.

As she ran back down the red carpet, her eyes stung and there was a solid lump lodged in her throat.

She'd expected something to shatter into a million pieces that night. She just hadn't expected it to be her heart.

* * *

The hotel suite was like a glass capsule, suspended mid-air over the lagoon, but if Alekos had expected a display of Kelly's normal exuberant enthusiasm then he was disappointed.

He'd caught up with her at the end of the red carpet and bundled her into the back of his waiting limousine, concerned that she hadn't appeared to be thinking about where she was going or what she was doing.

Once they'd arrived at the hotel, she'd stalked into the room ahead of him, tugged off her shoes and dropped them on the floor without giving him a backward glance. Now she had her hands behind her back, wriggling and writhing in an attempt to undo the invisible zip, clearly determined not to ask for his help.

She was seething; furiously angry.

Alekos strolled across to her and put his hands on her back, but she knocked him away.

'Don't touch me.' Her voice was shaking. 'On second thoughts, unzip this stupid dress so that I can take it off. I don't want to be wearing something made by one of your ex-girlfriends.'

Alekos took a deep breath. 'It did occur to me that you would be upset that the dress was by Marianna, which is why I didn't tell you.'

'It would have been better if you hadn't given me a dress by her in the first place!'

'I knew that red-carpet display would unnerve you.' He slid the zip down from neck to hem, feeling his body tighten as his eyes lingered on the smooth lines of her bare back. 'I thought it would help if you liked the way

you looked. Her clothes are highly sought-after, and I thought it would give you confidence to wear one of her unique creations.'

'Confidence?' She whirled round, her hair tumbling down from the elegant clip that had restrained it all evening. 'You think it gives me confidence to be told in public that I'm wearing a dress designed by your ex-girlfriend?'

'I did not know that Tatiana was going to make the connection.'

'Oh, well, that makes it fine, then!' Her voice thick with tears, Kelly yanked at the dress and pushed it off her body as if it were infectious. 'I see the label now.' She snatched the dress off the floor and stared at the elegant 'By Marianna' that had been discreetly hand-sewn onto a seam of the dress. 'I'm a complete and utter fool.'

Dragging his eyes from the generous curve of her creamy breasts, Alekos tried to focus. 'You are not a fool.' He breathed unsteadily but Kelly pushed her fists into her cheeks, her face crumpling as she struggled for control.

'Just get away from me. Only you can turn the most romantic city on earth into a hell hole.' Still dressed only in her underwear, Kelly stalked over to the window, hugging herself with her arms as she looked over the lagoon. 'That place is probably littered with the dead bodies of women who have thrown themselves in after spending a night with men like you.'

Raising his eyes to the ceiling, Alekos walked across to her. 'Marianna makes unique, elegant evening-dresses. She has a four-year waiting list because she is the best, and I wanted to buy you the best.'

Her shoulders stiffened a little more and she didn't turn. 'It was hideously insensitive.'

'I am with you, not her.'

'No, you're not—you're not with me, Alekos. Not really. We've just been going through the motions, haven't we?' She turned then, her face wet with tears, her mascara streaking under her eyes.

It occurred to Alekos that he'd never seen a woman cry properly before with no thought to her appearance. Instead of sniffing delicately, Kelly rubbed her face with her hand, smearing tears and mascara together. Alekos, who had never before been moved by tears, had never felt more uncomfortable in his life.

'We are *not* going through the motions.'

'Yes, we are. Have you ever said "I love you"? No, of course not, for the simple reason that you *don't* love me! I started off as someone to have sex with and ended up as someone having your baby—' Her voice hitched. 'And it's a *mess*. The whole situation is a horrid, tangled mess. And it's not supposed to be like this. It just isn't!' She started to sob but when Alekos put his hands on her shoulders she pushed him away roughly.

'You did it again. When Constantine asked you if you were a father, you said no!' Her face was wet, her eyes were red and swollen, but Alekos stood with his hands frozen to his sides, knowing that if he touched her she'd flip.

'Kelly...'

'No.' Her hair flew around her face as she shook her head. 'No more *excuses*. Do you know what, Alekos? I just can't do this. I can't carry on living on a knife edge, wondering whether this is going to be the day you tell me you can't do this any more. I don't want our child growing up wondering whether you're going to be there or not, feeling like he's done something wrong. You can't be there one minute and not the next, because I know how it feels to be standing on a doorstep waiting for a dad that never turns up!'

Transfixed into stillness by that revealing statement, Alekos stood watching her, waiting for Kelly to spill her guts as she always did and elaborate on the true reason behind her explosive reaction to his clumsy behaviour.

But tonight she just turned away from him and stared over the lagoon.

'I want to go h-home,' she sobbed. 'I want to go home to Little Molting. We'll sort the details out later.'

'You stood on a doorstep waiting? Is that what happened to you?' His voice was soft as he prompted her. 'Did your dad leave you waiting for him?'

She kept her back to him, her shoulders stiff. 'I don't want to talk about it.'

Alekos hung onto his own temper with difficulty. '*Theé mou*, you talk about everything else! There is not a single thing going on in your head that doesn't come out of your mouth, but this—' he gestured with a slice of his hand '—this really important thing, you don't mention to me. Why not?'

It was a moment before she answered. 'Because talking about it doesn't help,' she muttered. 'It doesn't make me feel nice.'

'Kelly.' Struggling to get it right, Alekos drew his hand over the back of his neck. 'Right this minute I'm not feeling nice, and I don't think you are either, so it would be great if you could just not pick this particular moment to clam up. Tell me about your father. I want to know. It's important.'

She rubbed her hand across her cheek and sniffed. 'My mum spent half her life trying to turn him into what she wanted him to be.'

'And what was that?'

'A husband. A father.' Her voice thick with tears, she kept wiping her eyes with her hand. 'But he didn't want children. Mum thought he'd come round to the idea, but he never did; that wasn't what happened. Occasionally his conscience would prick him and he'd phone to say he was coming to see me.' Her voice split. 'And I'd boast to all my friends that my dad was going to take me out. I'd pack my bag and wait by the door. And then he wouldn't turn up. That makes you feel pretty lousy, I can tell you. As childhoods went, it was no fairy tale.'

And she'd always wanted the fairy tale.

Thinking about his contribution to slashing those dreams, Alekos pressed his fingers to the bridge of his nose and tried to think clearly. 'Why didn't you tell me any of this before now?'

'Because it has nothing to do with us.'

'It has everything to do with us,' he said thickly. 'It explains a great deal about why you find it so hard to trust me. It explains why you keep giving me nervous looks. Why you keep waiting for me to fail.'

'The reason I keep giving you nervous looks is because I know this isn't what you wanted. And I know

that this sort of situation doesn't have a happy ending. We could keep it going for a while—maybe we'd split up and then get back together, who knows—but that isn't what I want, Alekos. I don't believe in the fairy tale any more,' she said in a faltering voice. 'But I do believe I deserve better than that. And so does my baby.' Without looking at him, she walked into the bedroom and closed the door.

Staring at that door, Alekos knew the gesture was symbolic.

She'd shut him out of her life.

Kelly dialled Vivien's number for the fourteenth time, left a fourteenth message and then ended the call.

She desperately needed to talk to someone, but her friend just wasn't answering the phone.

Scrabbling for a tissue, Kelly blew her nose. She had to stop crying. This was ridiculous; how much water could one person safely lose in twenty-four hours?

She'd been in no state to travel anywhere on her own so she'd agreed to travel back to Corfu and then back to London from there. And she'd cried for the whole duration of the flight. If the baby hadn't already scared Alekos off, then her tears would have done the trick, Kelly thought numbly, remembering Alekos's taut silence as he'd handed her tissue after tissue.

When he wasn't mopping up her tears, he'd worked, occasionally lifting his eyes from his emails to check on her.

Check that she wasn't about to go into meltdown.

But he hadn't attempted to resume the conversation they'd had the night before. He obviously thought she'd totally lost it, Kelly thought gloomily, remembering the look in his eyes as he'd watched her.

When she'd reminded him in a stiff voice that she wanted to return to England on the first available flight, he'd agreed to make arrangements, but the moment they'd arrived back at the villa he'd disappeared, presumably to his office to bury himself in work.

And now she was back in the master-bedroom suite, trying not to look at the enormous bed which dominated the beautiful room.

Switching off her brain, Kelly took a shower, dried her hair and then walked into her dressing room. She pulled on a pair of shorts and a simple tee-shirt and then tugged out her suitcase.

For a moment she stood, just looking at her clothes.

What use were any of those in Little Molting? She couldn't teach the children wearing pale-blue linen, could she?

And she couldn't wear any of the beautiful shoes unless Alekos was next to her, holding her arm.

Trying not to think about that, she walked back to the bedroom and instantly saw the note on the bed. Walking across the room, she picked it up, assuming it was her flight details: *meet me on the beach in ten minutes. Bring the ring.*

Of course. The ring.

Gritting her teeth against the tears that threatened, Kelly scrunched the note up and threw it in the bin. Great; so he wanted to make sure she didn't run off with his precious ring a second time.

She looked down at her hand, at the ring that had been with her on the bumpy journey that was her relationship with Alekos. The thought of parting with it just felt hideously sad.

Tugging it off her finger, she weighed it in her palm for a moment and bit her lip.

She had no idea why he wanted to meet her on the beach, but if that was what he wanted then that was what she'd do.

She'd deliver the ring to him in person for a final time.

Then she'd go back to her old life and try to learn to live without him.

Kelly walked slowly down the path, trying not to think about how perfect it would have been to bring up a child here, among the olive groves and the tumbling bougainvillea.

She felt as though someone had punched a hole through her insides. *As though she'd lost something that she'd never find anywhere else.*

Pausing for a moment, she closed her eyes. She just had to get through the next five minutes and that was it. She could go away and she'd never have to face him again.

Determined to be as dignified as possible, she walked onto the beach and stopped.

In front of her was a semi-circle of chairs, and in front of the chairs someone with flair and imagination had created an arch of flowers, a riot of colour that clung to the invisible wire-frame and created a door facing the sea.

It looked like a movie set for a very romantic wedding.

Which didn't make sense at all.

'Kelly?' Vivien's voice came from across the sand and then her friend was running towards her, her hair flying, her long dress tangling around her slim legs.

Laughing and crying at the same time, Kelly hugged her. 'I've been phoning you and phoning you—what on earth are you *wearing*?' She stood back from her friend and stared down at the dress in amazement. 'You look fantastic. Very glamorous. But—?'

'I'm your bridesmaid,' Vivien squeaked. 'He said it had to be a surprise so I switched my phone off, because you know I'm utterly useless at keeping secrets, and I knew if I spoke to you I'd give it away. Are you pleased?'

Kelly was confused. 'I—you look lovely, Vivien, but I—I don't need a bridesmaid. I'm not getting married.'

'What? Of course you are! Alekos flew me over here especially for your wedding. I had the whole private-jet experience.' Vivien grinned. 'I won't tell you how many mojitos I drank, but my head is killing me. Can we just get on with this?'

'You spoke your lines too early,' Alekos drawled from behind them. 'I was supposed to go first. She doesn't know anything about this.'

'What?' Vivien gaped at him. 'When you said it was a surprise, I assumed you meant that me being a bridesmaid was a surprise—not the whole wedding.'

'Things don't always go according to plan, and that is especially true of my relationship with Kelly.' Unusually

hesitant, Alekos took Kelly's hand in his. 'Last night, in Venice, I was going to ask you to marry me. That's why I took you there.'

Vivien gave a whimper and pressed her hand against her chest. 'Oh my.'

'Vivien.' Alekos was still looking at Kelly. 'If you open your mouth again before I give you permission, you will never travel on my private jet again.'

'Mmm.' Vivien made the sound through sealed lips, but Kelly was staring at Alekos.

'Y-you were going to ask me to marry you?' She shook her head. 'No! You were tense and edgy about the whole dress thing, and then when Constantine asked if you were a father you said no—you can't talk your way out of this one, Alekos.'

'I was tense and edgy because I was going to ask you to marry me and I was afraid you would turn me down,' he said huskily. 'After the last time, why would you trust me? I was gearing up to it for days. I took you to what I thought was one of the most romantic places on earth.'

'But—'

'All evening I was planning how to ask you, where would be best.'

'But Constantine?'

'Asked me if I was a father. I said no, because to me being a father is so much more than just creating a child. That's what your dad did, but he wasn't a father, was he?' His voice hoarse, he stroked his hands over her cheeks and cupped her face. 'Being a father is about loving your child more than you love yourself, putting their welfare before your own, protecting them from a

very hard world and making sure that they know that, whatever happens, you're there for them. And I can tell you that I'll do all those things, but it would mean more if I showed you. And that's going to take time.'

Kelly couldn't breathe. 'Time?'

'Let's start with fifty years or so.' His eyes scanned her face. 'We'll have to have quite a few children so that I get plenty of practice—at least four. And you can tell me how I'm doing. Maybe after fifty years and four children if someone asks if I'm a father I'll feel able to say yes.'

Kelly swallowed. 'I thought the whole idea scared you.'

'I didn't say I wasn't scared. I am. But I'm still standing here,' Alekos said softly. 'And I'm still holding your hand. And talking of hands...' He slid the ring off Kelly's hand and transferred it to the other hand.

Kelly felt her eyes mist. 'Alekos...'

'I love you, *agape mou*. I love you because you are generous, kind, funny and the sexiest woman I know. I love the fact you have to hold my arm because you can't walk in high heels; I love the fact you hate bits in your lemonade; I even love the fact that you drop your belongings everywhere.' He smoothed her hair away from her face. 'And I love the fact you would walk away from this relationship if it meant protecting our baby. But you don't have to do that, Kelly. We'll protect him—or her—together.'

Terrified to believe what was happening, Kelly stared down at the ring on her finger. 'You love me?'

'There is no question about that,' he said shakily. 'The only question is whether you can believe me, because

if you're always going to doubt me then this will never work. I'd like to think I'll never say the wrong thing to you, but I'm a man, so there's a fairly strong chance that at some point I'm going to get it wrong—like last night in Venice.' He spread his hands in a gesture of mute apology. 'I can see why you interpreted what I said that way, but—'

'You hadn't said you loved me,' Kelly muttered. 'You hadn't told me that. I was dying for you to tell me to move the ring back to my other hand, but you never did.'

A muscle flickered in his jaw. 'Kelly, four years ago I left you on your wedding day. That is a hard thing to forgive—we needed time, you know we did. I was afraid that if I asked you too soon you'd just refuse. I was *terrified* that you'd refuse. I was waiting.'

Kelly thought about the way their relationship had deepened over the past couple of months. 'I kept wanting you to ask. When you didn't, I assumed it was because you didn't love me.'

'I wanted you to be secure in the knowledge that I love you.'

'Alekos…'

'You have to know that, just because the wrong thing may have come out of my mouth, doesn't mean the right thing isn't in my heart.' Alekos lowered his head and kissed her, and for a long moment no one spoke.

Then Vivien cleared her throat. 'All right. Enough of this. It was pretty obvious to me that he loved you, Kel,' she said bluntly. 'I mean, you don't have any money of your own, you're rubbish at organisation, and although you can look pretty when you make an effort you're no

one's idea of a trophy wife because you haven't got that haughty look, and you fall over in high heels, so basically you don't have much going for you.'

'Thanks.'

'Which means it has to be love,' Vivien said airily. 'So can we get on with this before the bridesmaid gets sunburn?'

Half-laughing, half-crying, Kelly looked at Alekos. 'You want to get married right here? Now? I can't believe that you've arranged this on the beach—the flowers, the chairs.'

'I wanted to give you the fairy tale,' he said huskily. 'And, yes, we're doing it right now. I'm not going to change my mind, Kelly. I know what I want. And I think I know what you want. Neither of us need a crowd. If you say yes, then I have two people waiting in the villa—my head of legal, Dmitri, who also happens to be a close friend, and a man who is going to marry us.'

Caught in a whirlwind of happiness, Kelly gave a faltering smile. 'I can't get married wearing shorts.'

'Told you!' Vivien said triumphantly and she gestured to a pile of bags folded over a chair. 'Luckily for you, he's bought you a dress.'

Wondering if it was by Marianna, Kelly tensed, and Alekos gave a humourless laugh, reading her mind.

'No,' he said quietly. 'It isn't. In the name of honesty, I have to admit that I did order one, but that was before I knew it would upset you.' He breathed. 'I had ten different ones delivered to the villa this morning. You can choose something different.'

'Ten?' She stared at the pile on the chair. 'Ten.'

'I wanted you to have the choice.' A flicker of a smile touched his mouth. 'And I think you're supposed to surprise me.'

Touched by the thought behind the gesture, Kelly lifted her hand to his cheek. 'I love you. Thank you.' Tears spilled out of her eyes and Vivien gave a squeak of horror.

'Don't cry! You look hideous when you cry, and I'm supposed to do your make-up. There's not a lot I can do with super-red eyes. Go for a walk for half an hour, Alekos, so that I can get her into this dress. You're not supposed to see the bride—it's bad luck.'

'I could go to the villa,' Kelly protested, but Alekos shook his head.

'I'm not taking any chances,' he said huskily, lowering his mouth to hers again. 'I love you and I'm marrying you right now. I'd marry you in shorts.'

'Alekos Zagorakis, she is not wearing shorts! She has to drool over these wedding photos for the rest of her life, and no one can drool over a pair of shorts.' Outraged, Vivien gave him a push. 'All right, compromise—go and fetch your best man or whoever he is and come back in ten minutes.'

Ten minutes later, Kelly was standing under the arch of flowers, wearing the most beautiful dress she'd ever seen, gazing up at the only man she'd ever loved.

Vivien was making eyes at Dmitri.

'I have a feeling that neither your bridesmaid nor my best man are concentrating,' Alekos drawled, pulling Kelly against him, ignoring the disapproval of the man who was marrying them. 'We might have to do this without help.'

Kelly clutched the bunch of flowers that Vivien had pressed into her hands and smiled up at Alekos. 'I can't believe we're doing this at all. I didn't think it was going to end this way.'

'Does it feel like the fairy tale? Perhaps I should have laid on a couple of white horses and a carriage.'

She laughed. 'You'd never get a carriage down to this beach.' Standing on tiptoe, she kissed him. 'You got the important bits right.'

'We belong together,' he said huskily. 'For ever.'

Kelly smiled against his mouth. 'That sounds like the fairy tale to me.'

Coming Next Month

in **Harlequin Presents® EXTRA.** Available September 14, 2010.

Coming Next Month

in **Harlequin Presents®.** Available September 28, 2010.

LARGER-PRINT BOOKS!

PASSION GUARANTEED SEDUCTION

GET 2 FREE LARGER-PRINT NOVELS PLUS 2 FREE GIFTS!

YES! Please send me 2 FREE LARGER-PRINT Harlequin Presents® novels and my 2 FREE gifts (gifts are worth about $10). After receiving them, if I don't wish to receive any more books, I can return the shipping statement marked "cancel". If I don't cancel, I will receive 6 brand-new novels every month and be billed just $4.55 per book in the U.S. or $5.24 per book in Canada. That's a saving of at least 13% off the cover price! It's quite a bargain! Shipping and handling is just 50¢ per book.* I understand that accepting the 2 free books and gifts places me under no obligation to buy anything. I can always return a shipment and cancel at any time. Even if I never buy another book, the two free books and gifts are mine to keep forever.

176/376 HDN E5NG

Name	(PLEASE PRINT)

Address		Apt. #

City	State/Prov.	Zip/Postal Code

Signature (if under 18, a parent or guardian must sign)

Mail to the **Harlequin Reader Service:**
IN U.S.A.: P.O. Box 1867, Buffalo, NY 14240-1867
IN CANADA: P.O. Box 609, Fort Erie, Ontario L2A 5X3

Not valid for current subscribers to Harlequin Presents Larger-Print books.

Are you a subscriber to Harlequin Presents books and want to receive the larger-print edition?
Call 1-800-873-8635 today!

* Terms and prices subject to change without notice. Prices do not include applicable taxes. Sales tax applicable in N.Y. Canadian residents will be charged applicable provincial taxes and GST. Offer not valid in Quebec. This offer is limited to one order per household. All orders subject to approval. Credit or debit balances in a customer's account(s) may be offset by any other outstanding balance owed by or to the customer. Please allow 4 to 6 weeks for delivery. Offer available while quantities last.

Your Privacy: Harlequin Books is committed to protecting your privacy. Our Privacy Policy is available online at www.eHarlequin.com or upon request from the Reader Service. From time to time we make our lists of customers available to reputable third parties who may have a product or service of interest to you. If you would prefer we not share your name and address, please check here. ☐

Help us get it right—We strive for accurate, respectful and relevant communications. To clarify or modify your communication preferences, visit us at www.ReaderService.com/consumerschoice.

HPLP10R

HARLEQUIN®

A *Romance*

FOR EVERY MOOD™

Spotlight on

Inspirational

Wholesome romances
that touch the heart and soul.

See the next page
to enjoy a sneak peek from
the Love Inspired® inspirational series.

*See below for a sneak peek at
our inspirational line, Love Inspired®.
Introducing HIS HOLIDAY BRIDE
by bestselling author Jillian Hart*

Autumn Granger gave her horse rein to slide toward the town's new sheriff.

"Hey, there." The man in a brand-new Stetson, black T-shirt, jeans and riding boots held up a hand in greeting. He stepped away from his four-wheel drive with "Sheriff" in black on the doors and waded through the grasses. "I'm new around here."

"I'm Autumn Granger."

"Nice to meet you, Miss Granger. I'm Ford Sherman, from Chicago." He knuckled back his hat, revealing the most handsome face she'd ever seen. Big blue eyes contrasted with his sun-tanned complexion.

"I'm guessing you haven't seen much open land. Out here, you've got to keep an eye on cows or they're going to tear your vehicle apart."

"What?" He whipped around. Sure enough, mammoth black-and-white creatures had started to gnaw on his four-wheel drive. They clustered like a mob, mouths and tongues and teeth bent on destruction. One cow tried to pry the wiper off the windshield, another chewed on the side mirror. Several leaned through the open window, licking the seats.

"Move along, little dogie." He didn't know the first thing about cattle.

The entire herd swiveled their heads to study him curiously. Not a single hoof shifted. The animals soon returned to chewing, licking, digging through his possessions.

Autumn laughed, a warm and wonderful sound. "Thanks,

I needed that." She then pulled a bag from behind her saddle and waved it at the cows. "Look what I have, guys. Cookies."

Cows swung in her direction, and dozens of liquid brown eyes brightened with cookie hopes. As she circled the car, the cattle bounded after her. The earth shook with the force of their powerful hooves.

"Next time, you're on your own, city boy." She tipped her hat. The cowgirl stayed on his mind, the sweetest thing he had ever seen.

*Will Ford be able to stick it out in the country
to find out more about Autumn?
Find out in HIS HOLIDAY BRIDE
by bestselling author Jillian Hart,
available in October 2010
only from Love Inspired®.*

But it did exist.

It was as if just seeing him had flicked a switch inside her, reminded her what she was missing.

Too aware of his physical presence in her tiny hallway, Kelly walked through to the kitchen.

Alekos followed, this time bending his head to avoid the threat of the low beam. 'This house is a death trap.'

'For some, maybe. Perhaps it senses who is welcome and who isn't. It presents no threat to me whatsoever.'

But he did. Oh yes, *he* did. Just by being within a metre of her, he presented a threat.

It had always been like this between them. That searing awareness, an almost primal reaction that neither of them had ever felt before. The connection had created a fierce maelstrom of emotion from which neither of them had escaped unscathed. It had been scary, she admitted, to realise that such passion existed. Even now it was there, simmering between them like the precursor to a deadly storm. It didn't matter what had happened; she was learning to her cost that sexual attraction was no respecter of logic. 'Wait here. I'll get the ring.'

He glanced around the tiny room. 'Are you going to offer me coffee?'

'Why?'

His smile was barely discernible. 'Because it would be hospitable?'

'And hospitality is so important to you Greeks, isn't it? You'll leave a girl standing alone on her wedding day, but if you turn up uninvited in her home four years later you expect a cup of coffee and a slice of baklava.'

'I've never seen you angry before.'

'Stick around.' Kelly filled the kettle violently, squirting water down her front. 'On second thoughts, don't stick around.'

'Greek coffee, please.'

'I hate Greek coffee. You can have tea.'

He eyed the pot she'd abandoned on the work surface that morning. 'If you hate Greek coffee, why are you drinking it?'

Kelly stared at the offending pot, feeling her face redden. She could hardly tell him that she'd started drinking it because it had reminded her of the happy times they'd spent in Corfu, and that now she actually liked it. 'I—I—'

'It pleases me that you haven't turned your back on everything Greek.'

Making a point, Kelly turned her back on him; maybe it was childish but she didn't care. Pulling open a cupboard, she winced as a packet of rice fell on her head. Replacing it, she reached up and gingerly pulled out a jar of instant. 'This is what I usually drink,' she lied, removing the top with a twist of her wrist. She hadn't opened the jar for at least six months and the granules were stuck together. Gritting her teeth, she chipped at them with a spoon and then tipped them into a mug.

Observing this performance from beneath lustrous dark lashes, Alekos removed his jacket and slung it over the back of a kitchen chair. 'You always were a terrible liar.'

His arms were strong and muscled, and made her think about all the times she'd lain against his hard body, marvelling that this man was with her.

'Whereas you were a master of deceit. You could make love to a woman as if she was the only thing in your world, and then walk away the day of our wedding without so much as a goodbye.'

'Why did you sell the ring?'

Her mind was so firmly locked in the past that it took her a moment to shift to the present. They were having two different conversations, and she could feel the heat boiling under the surface of his bronzed skin. The same passion that had characterised their relationship now had a different focus. He simmered like a volcano waiting to erupt, his attention focused on her in a way that made her heart pound.

He was so physical, she thought weakly. The most physical man she'd ever met.

'Because I no longer have any use for it. It's just a reminder of a very bad decision. I'll get you that ring and then you can leave, preferably smacking your head on the way out.'

Her hands shaking, Kelly made his coffee and pushed it towards him, feeling a pang of guilt as the liquid sloshed over the sides. It went against her nature to be so inhospitable to a guest, but he wasn't a guest, was he? He was an intruder. And it was her nature that worried her. She knew herself too well to lower her guard. She didn't *dare* lower her guard, even for a moment. She was too aware of him for that—too aware of her reaction to him. It appalled her to realise that she could still find him shockingly attractive after what he'd done to her. She should not be noticing those thick, dark eyelashes or the dark stubble on his hard jaw. And she definitely should not be noticing the way his expensive shirt emphasised the width and power of his shoulders.

Instead she should remember how it had felt when all that leashed power had been focused on the destruction of their relationship.

Alekos paced the length of her kitchen, which for him took no more than three strides. Clearly it wasn't enough to relieve his simmering tension because he turned impatiently, dragging his hand through his hair in a gesture of frustration that was pure Mediterranean male. Or maybe not, Kelly thought wearily: the gesture was pure Alekos.

'That ring was a gift, and yet you were prepared to sell it to a stranger.' The words erupted from his throat and she stared at him in genuine amazement.

'Why would I keep it?' The ring weighed heavily against her chest. 'Do you think it holds some emotional meaning for me?'

'I gave it to you.'

'Payment for sex.' She wasn't going to let herself think it had been driven by anything else. 'That was all you ever wanted from me, wasn't it? All you think about is sex. Every minute of the day. That was all we ever shared.' Her reference to their passionate physical relationship made his eyes darken, and Kelly licked her lips, wishing she hadn't taken the conversation in that direction.

Mistake, she thought with a flash of panic. Big mistake.

'Not every minute. Every six seconds, is the opinion of experts.' Prowling restlessly around her kitchen, he looked brooding, virile and disturbingly male. 'Men think about sex every six seconds. Which leaves us five to think about other things.'

'Which for you is making money.'

'Are you short of money? Is that why you sold it?' Eyes stormy and menacing, he crossed the kitchen again, closing in on her.

She wasn't afraid of him, she told herself, gripping the work surface with her hands; she definitely wasn't. But there was something about his raw, elemental brand of masculinity that stirred her in a way that came close to terrifying. Being near him gave her a feeling she'd had with no other man and she didn't know if it was good or bad.

Bad, she thought, sucking air into her lungs. *Definitely bad*.

He was right in front of her now, legs spread apart, unapologetically male, his aura of rough sexuality sending the temperature in the room soaring to dangerous levels.

Her body aching with a need she'd suppressed for far too long, Kelly shoved at his chest with the flat of her hand. 'You're invading my personal space, Alekos. Get away from me.'

'I've spent the last five seconds thinking about coffee,' he said silkily, 'Which means I've now moved onto sex.'

She was stupid, stupid to have mentioned sex to this man.

She didn't want to think about sex while she was in the same room as him. It was the one topic they should have avoided. The most dangerous.

But it was already too late.

The heat was spreading through her pelvis, slow and insidious, stealing through her like smoke from a fire. And the fire was raging, curling inside her, ready to burn up everything in its path.

Fighting that reaction, Kelly pushed past him, but he caught her arm and hauled her against him. Their bodies collided with an almost fatal inevitability, and in that single, highly charged instant he read her body. As sure as if he'd stripped her naked, he knew what she was feeling. He'd always known, even before she'd known herself.

That intimate knowledge hovered between them, as acute as it was unwelcome.

Without warning, his mouth came down on hers, hard and demanding. She was dragged back four years, sucked back into a time when passion had ruled thought, when the world had been a perfect place, and when the only thing that had mattered was being with this man.

For a moment she melted. She couldn't breathe or think.

Swamped, Kelly struggled to free herself and dragged her mouth from his. 'No!'

She heard him draw a ragged breath, his eyes blazing into hers as he tried to focus. 'You're right.' His usually accent less English was thickened and pronounced. 'It is crazy.'

'I don't—' Her mouth was burning. Her body was on fire.

'Neither do I.'

If either of them had stepped back, they might have stood a chance.

Instead their mouths collided again with almost brutal force. The raw chemistry that exploded between them was so intense that for a moment she couldn't help herself.

She'd missed this.

She'd missed *him*.

Missed the feel of his mouth. The touch of his hands. Kelly kissed him back hungrily, her mouth every bit as greedy as his, her tongue every bit as bold. But there was anger in her kiss too, and as she felt his response to her she thought, *just look at what you're missing: just look at what you gave up.*

He muttered something in Greek, so shaken that she felt a vicious rush of satisfaction.

Yes, she thought, *it was good and you threw it away. You threw* this *away.*

Purring in her throat, she licked at the corner of his mouth, the caress dangerously provocative. She had no idea what was pushing her—desire? Pride? Revenge? All she knew was that she wanted to be with him again. Just this once.

Without breaking the kiss, Alekos powered her back against the work surface, jabbed his fingers into her hair and gripped her head. Her fingers were locked in the front of his shirt, dragging him closer. They kissed as if it were their last moment on the planet, as if the future of civilisation depended on their desire for each other, *as if they had never parted.*

Kelly was so turned on she ignored the thought that this was really, really stupid.

His touch was as skilled as she remembered—his kisses as bone-meltingly perfect.

Yes, she was angry with him—blisteringly angry— but that just seemed to intensify the emotions that flared between them. Anger was just another fuel to stoke a fire that was already white-hot. She didn't want to feel like this, but sex had never been the problem between them, had it? Maybe that was why she'd given it up, she thought as she dug her fingers into the hard muscle of his shoulders. She'd known it could never be like this with anyone else. Celibacy had been preferable to disappointment.

'*Theé mou*, we should not be doing this.' He growled the words against her throat and she gasped and slid her leg around his, unwilling to let him go.

'You're right. We shouldn't.'

'You're angry.'

'Boiling mad.'

'I'm *furious* that you sold the ring.'

'I'm furious you're giving it to another woman.'

'I'm not!' He jerked her head back, his gaze black and intense, his voice thickened by the swirly, sultry atmosphere. 'I'm *not* giving it to another woman.'

'I hate her. I hate *you*.'

He breathed in deeply. 'I probably deserve that.'

'You definitely deserve it.' But her hands were on his belt and she heard the breath hiss through his teeth as her fingers brushed against the hard, rigid length of him.

'If we do this, you will hate me even more than you do already.'

'Trust me, that isn't possible.'

His hand slid up her thigh, hooking her leg higher. 'In that case, there is no incentive to stop.' He groaned as his fingers touched bare legs. 'You're wearing stockings?'

'I always wear stockings for work.' *Does* she *wear stockings, Alekos? Does she do this to you? Does she make you feel this way?*

'Stockings under that prim black skirt.' The prim black skirt hit the floor. 'The whole teacher-outfit thing really turns me on.' He dragged the clip out of her hair, silencing her gasp of pain with his mouth. 'Sorry. Sorry. I didn't meant to hurt you.'

'You always hurt me.' Her hair was all around them and she could feel his hands buried into the soft mass, his fingers biting into her scalp. 'In the scheme of things, a little more pain doesn't count.'

'I know I was a complete bastard.'

'Yes, you were—still are. And now could you please just—?' Rocking her hips against him, she sank her teeth into his lip and Alekos took her mouth hungrily, his hands now locked against her bottom.

'No other woman has ever made me feel the way you make me feel.'

The words sent a thrill of satisfaction through her. 'But I'm sure you've kept looking.'

He buried his face in her neck. 'You were never this wild four years ago.'

She was never this desperate. Kelly's eyes closed. 'Don't talk.'

His answer was to weld his mouth to hers again and kiss her until she couldn't breathe or stand upright. Her hands closed over his shoulders, but what began as a need for support, ended in a caress as her fingers slid over hard, male muscle.

'Kelly...'

'Shut up.' She didn't want to talk about what they were doing. She wasn't sure she even wanted to think about it. Her teeth gritted, she ripped his shirt so that she could get to his chest, hair tickling her fingers as she slid her hands over the hard muscle of his chest. His tie still hung between them but she ignored it, too absorbed by his body to bother undressing him.

To have sex with Alekos was to understand why her body had been invented.

His eyelids were lowered, his eyes half-shut as he watched her. It was a look of such raw, sexual challenge that she shivered.

Later, she thought, I'm going to really regret this.

But right now she didn't care.

He was probably lying about the ring. He was probably going to give it away, but she was going to make sure that he didn't forget *her*, Kelly thought as she trailed her mouth over his jaw, feeling the roughness of stubble graze her lips. Other women had sex with men they didn't know. She'd never done that; for her, sex had begun and ended with this man.

She was achy, needy, and when he backed her to the table and lifted her she just gave a groan of assent, closing her fingers around the glorious velvet length of him.

'Alekos...'

'I need to taste you, I need to...' Muttering something in Greek, he ripped at her shirt, tore at her bra and fastened his mouth over her breast.

Kelly's head fell back, the heat of his mouth like a brand. She squirmed as hot, liquid pleasure pumped through his veins and he lifted his head and devoured her mouth again, both of them crazily out of control.

'Now!' She yanked at his tie, pulling him towards her, and he flattened her to the table and pushed her thighs up. Dragging aside her panties, he entered her in a single, driving thrust that had her crying out his name. It had been so long that it took her a moment to adjust to the size of him. He was hard, full and pulsing hot, and Kelly held herself rigid, afraid to breathe or move. And then his mouth claimed hers again and from then on it was wild, each rhythmic thrust driving away all thoughts of how much she hated him—the fact that this was going to turn out to be a bad decision. He wrapped her thighs around his hips and she dug her nails into his back as she matched his demands with her own.

It was so shockingly good that when his phone buzzed there was no question of him answering it; neither of them were capable of focusing on anything but each other. He had one hand locked in her hair, the other under her bottom, anchoring her in a position designed to give them both maximum pleasure. He thrust hard, fast, his movements so unerringly skilful that she felt her body erupt with sensation. After four years it was never going to last long, and when she felt the first ripples take hold of her she moaned his name. Exquisite pleasure bordered on pain; his fingers tightened in her hair and his mouth locked on hers as he drove them both higher.

They were kissing when the explosion took them. Wave after wave engulfed them, crashing down on them, leaving no room for breath or recovery as they were caught in the web of sensation they'd spun for themselves. They kissed through her choked gasps and through his tortured groan, through the contractions that racked both of them and left them shaken.

His chest was slick against hers, his fingers still digging hard into her bottom as he dragged in air.

Kelly lay stunned, deliciously aware of the weight of him, the *feel* of him. If she'd been young and naive, she might have thought that such incredible sex could only happen when there was love, but she wasn't a naive teenager any more.

Slowly recovering her powers of thought, she realised with a flash of horror that the ring was round her neck. Panicking, Kelly pushed him away and fastened the few remaining buttons on her shirt with hands that shook.

Had he noticed?

No; both of them had been too carried away to notice anything but each other. Even if the ring had bashed him in the face, she doubted he would have seen it.

And now she had to get him out of here before she made a fool of herself. 'I'll get you the ring,' she croaked, walking to the door without looking over her shoulder. Her legs were shaking and her body was on fire but she knew she didn't dare think about what they'd just shared. Not yet. Not now. Later—when she was on her own.

Up in her bedroom, she unfastened the gold chain she wore around her neck and slid the ring into her palm. It glinted and winked at her and she felt a lump build in her throat. It had been next to her skin for four years. It had witnessed her pain and her slow, faltering recovery. Giving it back should feel cathartic—that was the theory.

The practice was something quite different.

Hearing a sound from the hall, Kelly quickly wiped her eyes on the back of her hand and walked back down the stairs.

The front door was wide open.

'Alekos?' Puzzled, she glanced from the open door to the kitchen and then heard the unmistakeable, throaty growl of an impossibly powerful engine.

Sprinting to the door, the ring still in her hand, she watched in disbelief as the Ferrari roared away.

CHAPTER FOUR

'OK, BREATHE, breathe...I always seem to be saying that to you; how come you have so much drama in your life? I'm having an exciting day if my card doesn't work in the cash machine.' Juggling a half-eaten tub of chocolate ice cream and a box of tissues, Vivien sat on the sofa next to Kelly. 'How can you be pregnant? You haven't had sex for four years. Even elephants don't take that long.'

Kelly tried to fight her way through the panic. 'I had sex three weeks ago.'

Ice cream and spoon fell to the carpet. 'You had sex *three weeks* ago? But you don't—I mean, who with? You never go out. You're not the one-night-stand type—and three weeks ago was when Alekos...' Vivien's smile faltered and Kelly wrapped her arms around herself, feeling her face heat.

'Yes.' Just admitting it made her want to shrink. *What had she been thinking?*

'Alekos?'

'Can you stop saying his name? I seem to remember you being happy enough when he was kissing me.'

'That was a kiss! Last time I checked, a kiss couldn't make you pregnant! Alekos? This is the guy you hate, the guy who ruined your life.' Vivien grabbed a handful of tissues and tried to mop up the worst of the ice cream. 'What an unbelievable mess.'

'I know that.'

'I meant my carpet, not your life—although your life isn't looking too great, either.' Covered in chocolate ice cream, Vivien licked her fingers. 'So is that why he walked out without taking the ring?'

'I don't know. I suppose so, but he didn't talk to me, so I don't know. He just vanished. As usual.' Increasingly agitated, Kelly sprang up and walked around Vivien's tiny living-room.

'Kel.' Vivien's voice was firm. 'It's not that I don't love you or that I don't care deeply about your trauma, but would you mind *awfully* not treading on the bit with the ice cream? You'll walk it all around the flat, and my landlord is going to shred me if the place is covered in chocolate footprints.'

'Sorry.' Kelly stood still, rubbing her hands over her arms, trying to warm herself up. She felt sick; was that pregnancy or panic? 'Sorry. I'll help you clean it up.'

'Forget it. I'll squirt something on it in the morning.' Covering the stain with a cloth, Vivien flung herself in the chair and picked up the tub again. 'So, you don't speak to the guy for four years and then suddenly you have passionate sex. I'm seeing a whole different side to you. I honestly never thought of you as—'

'Sex mad? Sex starved? Maybe this is what happens when you keep men at a distance for too many years. Oh God, what was I thinking, Vivi? He dumps me—' her voice rose '—and what do I do? I reward him by having sex with him. What is the matter with me? Am I sick?'

Vivien eyed her warily. 'I hope not because my carpet has taken enough punishment. How many years?'

'What?'

'You said this is what happens when you keep men at a distance for too many years. How long actually is it since you last had sex?'

Distracted, Kelly racked her brains. 'I think it was about four years ago. Just after—it was part of my Alekos rehabilitation-programme.'

'I gather it didn't work.'

Kelly took slow, deep breaths, trying to calm herself so that she could think clearly. 'Have you ever had a relationship where you just can't help yourself? You *know* it isn't good for you, you know there is going to be agony at the end of it, but something between you is so powerful it just draws you together.'

'No. But my sister-in-law is an alcoholic and that description sounds uncannily close to how she feels about a bottle of vodka.'

'I don't find that analogy comforting. If she went without vodka for four years, would she still feel like that?'

'Oh yes. She says the feeling never goes away. It's just a question of not putting yourself near the vodka.'

'The vodka took me home and barged into my house.'

Vivien blinked. 'This conversation is getting too complicated for me. But vodka sounds like a good idea. I have some somewhere, for emergencies.'

'I'm pregnant,' Kelly said in a high voice. 'I can't drink.'

'But I can. I'll drink for both of us while you decide what you're going to do.' Moments later, Vivien emerged from the tiny kitchen carrying a bottle, her face white.

'Forget that. You don't need to decide what to do, it's been taken out of your hands. There's an enormous limousine outside my flat and I don't know anyone who owns one.'

'*What?*'

'It's Alekos; it has to be.'

'No!' Panicking, Kelly sprang to her feet. 'It can't be him. Why would he be here? He can't know I'm pregnant.'

'Well, he *was* present at the time of conception,' Vivien said helpfully. 'And he obviously has a planet-sized brain, so there is a possibility that he's considered that as a potential outcome.'

Her breath coming in rapid pants, Kelly pressed her hand to her chest. 'No. *No.*'

'On the other hand, men are a bit thick sometimes, so it's always possible that he's just come for the ring.' Vivien patted her shoulder soothingly. 'In which case, he's going to be leaving with something that's going to cost him a whole load more by the time you've added up nappies, clothes, an iPod and all the stuff kids seem to need now. Then there's university fees, and—'

'Shut *up*, Viv! You can't let him in. Don't let him in. I haven't decided what to do.' Kelly was panicking badly. 'I need time.'

'Don't be ridiculous! Time isn't going to change anything but your age.' Vivien sprang towards the door. 'But I promise not to say, "hello, Daddy". Or "did you bring the nappies?"'

Kelly sank back onto the sofa with her head in her hands. Was she going to tell him? Of course she was going to tell him. She couldn't deny her child the right to know his father, could she? That wasn't her decision to make.

Maybe they could be one of those couples who seemed to get on perfectly well but just didn't live together. But that would mean shuffling her child backwards and forwards like a lost parcel, and she didn't want to do that.

Kelly groaned and pressed her hand to her forehead. How had this complete and utter nightmare happened to her? If only she hadn't sold the ring, he wouldn't have come looking for her, they wouldn't have had sex and she wouldn't be pregnant.

Just thinking of the word made her shake.

She needed time to think. She wasn't ready to do this now.

The door to Vivien's flat banged. 'You can relax, it isn't him. It's one of his slaves.' Vivien came in dragging a small suitcase and thrust an envelope at her. 'Here we are. You can tip me if you like; round it up to the nearest million.'

'What's that? And where did you get that suitcase?' Kelly slit the letter open and immediately recognised Alekos's bold, dark scrawl. Reading the letter, she gulped.

'Now what?' Vivien snatched the letter from her: *My private jet is waiting for you at the airport. Jannis will drive you. I will see you in Corfu.* 'Kel, any minute now I'm going to poke you in the eye with something sharp. Four-million-dollar diamond rings, Ferraris, limousines, private jets—give me one reason why I shouldn't die of envy?'

Kelly's teeth were chattering. 'The guy left me on my wedding day.'

'True. But honestly, Kelly, private jet,' Vivien said weakly. 'I mean, I bet you get loads of leg room. And the person in front won't recline his seat into your face. No plastic food. How quickly could I get breast implants? I could go instead of you.'

'You can go instead of me if you like because I'm not going.' Kelly stared at the suitcase. 'What's that?'

'Jannis said it was for you.'

'Jannis? You're on first-name terms? You got friendly rather quickly.' Kelly dropped onto her knees and opened the suitcase.

'Oh my goodness—clothes wrapped in tissue paper.' Vivien's voice was faint as she peered over Kelly's shoulder. 'He's bought you a *wardrobe*?'

'Probably because he doesn't want me to show him up arriving dressed in my completely embarrassing black skirt,' Kelly said stiffly, ripping apart tissue paper and pulling out a dress. 'Oh! It's—'

'*Gorgeous*. Is that silk?'

Kelly fingered the beautiful fabric wistfully and then she stuffed it back in the suitcase. 'No idea. Send it back to Jannis.'

'*What?* Kelly, he's inviting you to Corfu. You have to go.'

'He wants me to bring his ring, that's why! I'm his personal delivery-service and this is my payment.'

Vivien was still poking through the contents. 'It's a pretty good payment; these shoes are Christian Louboutin—do you know how much they cost?'

Kelly eyed the height of the heel in disbelief. 'No, but I know the surgery to fix my broken ankle would be a lot. Not to mention all the things I'll probably smash to pieces as I fall trying to walk in those. Vivien, I'm *not* going.'

Vivien folded her arms, a stubborn look on her face. 'If this is about that woman he was seeing, he's not with her any more. I've already told you that. It was all over the papers that they'd split up. Now I know why. He shagged you and realised that you're the only one.'

'If that's supposed to sound romantic, you need to try harder.' But there was no denying that, ever since she'd heard the news that Alekos had parted from that Marianna woman, her mood had lifted. It had been like walking in the darkness and suddenly discovering that you had a torch in your pocket.

'You're pregnant. You're having this man's baby. He has a right to know.'

Kelly's palms were suddenly damp with sweat. 'I *will* tell him.'

'And this is the perfect time. Look at it this way: you tell him about the baby, then you can have a holiday in Greece with the four-million dollars.'

Kelly swallowed, her eyes on the suitcase. 'I think I'd find it hard going back to Corfu.' Everything had happened there. She'd fallen in love. *She'd had her heart broken.*

'Life's hard,' Vivien said in a brisk, practical tone. 'But it's a heck of a lot easier if you have four-million dollars, and at least you're going to face the world wearing Christian Louboutin.'

'I don't think they'll fit over a plaster cast.'

'You hold his arm while you wear them. That's why you have a man.'

'I don't have a man.'

Vivien sighed. 'Yes, you do. You're just not sure if you want him. But look at it this way, Kel—the school holidays start tomorrow and your alternative is being sad and lonely here. Better to be rich and angry in Greece. Go. Put on the dress and the heels and walk right over him.'

* * *

Mistake, mistake, mistake...

Kelly sat rigid in the back of the chauffeur-driven car, staring straight ahead as they drove through the middle of bustling Corfu town, up across the mountains that rose in the centre of the island and down through twisty, narrow roads that led through endless olive groves. Each turn in the road revealed another tantalising glimpse of sparkling, turquoise sea and buttercup-yellow sand but Kelly was too stressed to enjoy the scenic temptations of Greece.

On her first trip to this island she'd fallen in love with the place, loving the smells, the sounds and the bright colours that were Greece. Then she'd fallen in love with the man.

Kelly felt nerves explode in her stomach.

If she'd arrived here under different circumstances, she would have been excited and thrilled. Instead she could hardly breathe. Anxiety choked her and all she could feel was panic at the thought of seeing Alekos again.

They hadn't seen each other since that day in her kitchen.

She didn't even know why she'd come. Not really.

Licking dry lips, she stared out of the window. Why had he asked her to bring the ring in person? What was going on in his head? What was he thinking?

Her brain was careering forward like a wild ride at a theme park. One minute hope popped up and she felt a flash of optimism, and then she was confronted by the ugly memory of what he'd done and hope plummeted to earth like a meteorite, leaving her drained and pessimistic.

She couldn't forget that one comment he'd made about him doing her a favour by not marrying her. It had played over and over again in her head during the weeks since he'd walked out of her house, leaving the door wide open.

What exactly had he meant by that?

Was he implying that she'd been too young or something? Kelly gnawed her lip as she stared out of the window. Nineteen *was* pretty young to get married. Perhaps he'd been worried she hadn't seen enough of the world or that she hadn't known her own mind.

The only thing she knew for sure was that she had no idea what was going on in *his* mind, and she needed to know. She needed to know what future there was for her and her baby.

Resting her hand low on her abdomen, Kelly made herself a promise.

Whatever happened, however this turned out, there was one thing she was sure about: she was *not* going to do what her mother had done. She wasn't going to cling onto a relationship that was never going to work.

This wasn't just about her any more. It was about her child.

And she knew how it felt to be the child of parents who absolutely shouldn't have been together.

As the car drove through a pair of elaborate wrought-iron gates, Kelly felt her stomach drop with anticipation. Even the novelty of having a private jet to herself hadn't been able to damp down her apprehension at the approaching meeting. Whatever Alekos was expecting, it probably wasn't the news that she was pregnant.

A stomach-churning cocktail of excitement and dread formed inside her.

Maybe he'd be pleased, she thought optimistically, hunting around for evidence to support that theory.

Alekos was Greek, wasn't he? Everyone knew that Greeks had big families. Everyone knew the Greeks loved children. Unlike their counterparts in England, who had a tendency to treat the arrival of children with the same enthusiasm as vermin, Greek restaurant-owners were delighted when a young family arrived on the premises. They smiled indulgently if children ran around and danced to the music. Family was the Greek way of life.

And that was her dream, wasn't it? The whole 'big family' thing.

That was what she'd always wanted.

Despite her efforts to keep her mind in check, Kelly's thoughts drifted off on a tangent as she imagined what Christmas would be like with lots of small versions of Alekos dragging out prettily wrapped parcels from under the enormous tree. It would be noisy, chaotic, a bit like a day in her classroom, which was one of the reasons she loved teaching. She loved the noisy, busy atmosphere that was created when lots of children were together.

Maybe Alekos felt the same way.

Kelly gave a tiny frown. It was true that Alekos had talked to her class as if he'd been in a board meeting, but he probably just needed practice, didn't he? He needed to understand that he couldn't apply the principles of corporate management to child rearing. He was basically Greek, so that whole 'family' thing should be welded into his DNA.

Maybe, just maybe, they could make this work.

At the very least, they had to try.

How could she ever look her child in the eye and say that she hadn't even tried?

The limousine pulled up in a large courtyard dominated by a fountain, and Kelly gulped. The first time
she'd seen Alekos's Corfu home, she'd been shocked
into awed silence by the sheer size and elegance of the
villa. As someone who had grown up in a small house,
she'd found the space and luxury of his Mediterranean
hideaway incredibly intimidating.

She still did.

Reminding herself not to scatter her possessions
around his immaculate villa, Kelly stepped hesitantly
out of the car.

'Mr Zagorakis has instructed me to tell you that he
is finishing a conference call and will meet you on the
terrace in five minutes.' Jannis urged her inside the villa
and Kelly gazed around at the familiar interior, no less
daunted now than she'd been four years earlier.

The floors of the villa were polished marble and
Kelly picked her way nervously, relieved she hadn't
worn the Christian Louboutin shoes. *Death by stilettos,* she thought uneasily, wishing Alekos had installed
a handrail. Maybe the Greek aristocracy were given
lessons in skating in heels when they were children.

Cautiously eyeing the priceless antiques, she kept
her hands pressed to her sides, terrified that she was
going to bang into something and send it smashing into
a zillion pieces on the mirror floors. Nothing was out
of place. Everything looked as though it was where it
was supposed to be: no magazines, no half-read books,
no unopened letters or junk mail covered in pictures of
pizza, no half-drunk mugs of tea.

Feeling as though she was in a museum, Kelly looked
round nervously, relieved when Jannis led her through a
curved archway that led onto the terrace. No matter how
many times she saw the view, it still made her gasp.

The beautiful gardens fell away beneath her, hot-pink oleander and bougainvillea tumbling down the gentle slope to the curve of perfect beach that nestled below the villa.

Kelly blinked in the sudden brightness of the midday sun, watching as a yacht drifted silently across the spar-kling sea. She felt slightly disconnected, unable to be-lieve that yesterday she'd woken up in her bed in Little Molting and now she was back on the island of Corfu with the sun shining in her eyes.

A lump settled in her throat.

She'd left her dreams here, on a sandy beach, with the sound of the sea in the air.

'Was your journey comfortable?' His voice was deep, dark and husky, and Kelly froze, desperately conscious that this was the first time she'd seen him since that day in her kitchen. A sizzle of sexual awareness shot through her body and her tongue stuck to the roof of her mouth as she turned.

The air was electric. If either one of them had touched the other, that would have been it. The dangerous glitter of his eyes said it all, and Kelly felt her body grow heavy with longing.

Suddenly she wished there were other people in the villa. She needed someone else to dilute the concentra-tion of sexual tension that threatened to drown both of them.

She didn't *want* to drown. She wanted to think with her head, not react with her body.

Trying to apply caution, Kelly reminded herself that this was nothing like the last time. She'd grown up, hadn't she?

Her own particular fairy tale had most definitely *not* had a happy ending.

'The journey was fine. I've never been on a private jet before. It was, well, private.' She winced as she listened to herself. *Oh for goodness' sake, Kelly, say something more intelligent than that.* But her tongue had apparently wrapped itself into an elaborate knot and her heart was racing at a very unnerving pace. 'It felt a bit weird, if I'm honest.'

Bold dark brows rose in question. 'Weird?'

Kelly shrugged awkwardly. 'It was a bit lonely. And your hostess woman wasn't very chatty.'

A smile touched the corner of his mouth, that same shockingly sensual mouth that knew how to drive a woman from wild to crazy. 'She is not paid to chat. She's paid to make sure you have whatever you need.'

'I needed a chat.'

Alekos breathed deeply. 'I will make sure someone speaks to her about being more, er, *chatty.*'

'No, don't do that; I don't want to get her into trouble or anything, I'm just saying it wasn't as much fun as I thought it would be. There's not a lot of point travelling in a private jet if there isn't anyone to laugh about it with, is there?'

A look of incredulity crossed his handsome features and it was clear he'd never given the matter consideration before. 'The point,' he drawled, 'is that you have the space and privacy to do whatever you want to do.'

'But no one to do it with.' Realising that she probably sounded really ungrateful, Kelly tried to retrieve the situation. 'But it was great not having to queue through customs, and brilliant to be able to lie flat on the sofa.'

'You lay *flat*?'

'So I didn't crease my dress.' Kelly smoothed the fabric, wondering why something so simple as a dress could make you feel good. 'It's linen, and I didn't want to arrive looking as though I'd jumped out the laundry basket. The clothes are great, by the way; thanks. How did you know I had nothing to wear?'

'I didn't. It was a guess.'

Kelly gave an awkward laugh. 'Good guess. My wardrobe is full of stuff that doesn't fit me any more, but I refuse to throw it away because one day I'm going to be a size zero.'

His gaze slid down her body and lingered on her breasts. 'I sincerely hope not.'

That look was all it took. Her breasts tingled and her nipples pressed against the fabric of her dress, defying all her attempts to control her reaction. Not wanting to look down at herself and risk drawing attention to what was happening, Kelly fumbled with the clasp of her purse and pulled out the ring. 'Here. This is yours. This must be the most expensive delivery-service ever, but here you go.' She held out the enormous diamond, frowning when he made no move to take it. 'Well? Go on—it's yours.'

'I gave it to you.'

'Not exactly. I mean, you *did*, but it was supposed to come with a wedding. And, anyway, you bought it back from me,' Kelly reminded him. 'For four-million dollars. And, if you're waiting for me to say I'd rather have the ring than the money, forget it. I've already given away a big chunk of it to pay for the new playground. I can't give you the money back, so you have to take the ring. A better person than me probably wouldn't have taken the ring *or* the money, but I've discovered I'm not a better person. Exposure to wealth has obviously warped me.'

Alekos studied her, a curious look in his intense dark eyes, a smile flickering around his sensual mouth. 'You suddenly find yourself with four-million dollars and you spend the money on a new playground? I think you might need some lessons on the true motivation of the gold-digger, *agape mou*.'

Even though she hated to admit it, the endearment made her heart flutter. Or maybe it was his voice—deep, sexy and chocolate-smooth. This whole thing would be easier, Kelly thought desperately, if she wasn't so drawn to him. It was difficult to push something away when you wanted it more than anything.

The tips of her fingers tingled with the desire to touch, and she linked her hands behind her back to be on the safe side. 'I didn't spend *all* the money, obviously. What use is a gold-plated playground? But I found this brilliant climbing-frame—massive—and it comes with this bit that's like a tree house…' Nervous and unsettled, she faltered. *Don't bore him, Kelly.* 'Never mind. Take it from me, it's a good one. And we're having this special surface put down over the summer holidays so that if the kids fall they shouldn't break anything…' Her voice tailed off and she shrugged self-consciously. 'Don't say anything to them. I pretended I was an anonymous benefactor.'

'They don't know the money came from you?'

'No.' A grin spread across her face as she remembered the staff meeting. 'They were all guessing. It feels good giving money away to good causes, doesn't it? It makes you go all warm and fuzzy inside. I guess you get that feeling all the time when you give stuff away.'

'I don't give anything away personally. Charitable donations are managed by the Zagorakis Foundation.'

Kelly digested that information with astonishment. 'You mean you have a whole company that gives away your money?'

'That's right. It was set up for that purpose. We donate a proportion of income, and they analyse all the applications and make a decision—with my input.'

'But you don't actually get to meet the people you help?'

'Sometimes. Not usually.'

'But don't you feel warm and fuzzy when you know you've helped someone?'

Alekos studied her through heavy-lidded dark eyes. 'I can't honestly say that "warm and fuzzy" features large in my emotional repertoire.'

'Oh. Well, it should, because you've obviously helped loads of people so you *should* feel good about that.' It was confusing, thinking about that side of him. Or maybe it was just the man himself who was confusing. Experience was telling her to be wary, but instinct was telling her to throw herself into his arms. It was probably because he was standing so close. He smelt fantastic, Kelly thought weakly, thrusting the ring towards him again.

'Are you going to take this? It sort of freaks me out, holding it, knowing how much it is worth. It's a good job I didn't know it was that valuable when I owned it. I never would have left the house.'

'Put it on your finger.'

Kelly's eyes flew to his and for a moment everything around her ceased to exist. Had he said...? Did he mean...? Even before her brain had answered the question, her heart performed a happy dance all on its own. He couldn't possibly mean that, could he? He couldn't be proposing...

'W-what did you say?'

'I want you to wear it.' His hands sure and decisive, Alekos took the ring from her and slid it onto the third finger of her right hand.

Her right hand.

Kelly felt the hard slug of disappointment deep in her gut and suddenly she was cross with herself. What was the matter with her? Even if he *had* proposed, she would have said no, wouldn't she? After what happened last time, she wasn't just going to walk back into his arms, no questions asked. No way.

'It looks good there,' Alekos said huskily, and Kelly bit back the impulse to tell him that it had looked even better on her left hand.

The diamond winked and flashed in the bright sunlight, dazzling her as much now as it had four years before. Reminding herself that a diamond didn't make a marriage, she yanked it off her finger before her brain could start getting the same silly ideas as her body. 'I've told you, I've already spent the money. I don't want the ring. I don't understand what's going on. I don't know why I'm here.' Which probably said more about her than him, she thought gloomily: he'd summoned her and she'd come running.

'I wanted to talk to you. There are things that need to be said.'

Kelly thought about the child growing inside her and decided that had to be the understatement of the century. 'Yes.' She squeezed her hand around the ring, feeling the stone cutting into her palm. 'I have a couple of things to say to you, too. Well, one thing in particular—nothing that…' Suddenly she felt horribly nervous about his reaction. What was the best way to tell him—straight out? Lead up to it with a conversation about families and kids? 'It's something pretty important, but it can wait. You go first.' She needed more time to build up her courage. She needed someone like Vivien bolstering her up from the sidelines.

She needed to stop thinking about her own child-hood.

'Put the ring back on your finger, at least for now. I'll pour you a drink—you look hot.' Alekos strolled over to a small table which had been laid by the beautiful pool. 'Lemonade?'

Still rehearsing various ways to spill her own piece of news, Kelly was distracted. 'Oh, yes please. That would be lovely.' Wondering what on earth he wanted to say to her, Kelly slid the ring back on the finger of her right hand as a temporary measure. They could argue about it later. 'So, I read in the papers that you broke up with your girlfriend. I'm sorry about that.'

'No, you're not.' A smile touched his mouth as he poured lemonade into two chilled glasses, ice clinking against the sides.

'All right, I'm trying to *feel* sorry, because I don't want to be a bad person. And I do feel sorry for her, in a way. I feel sorry for any woman who has been dumped by you. I know how it feels. Sort of like missing your step at the top of the stairs and finding yourself crashing to the bottom.'

He winced as he handed her a glass. 'That bad?'

'It feels as though you've broken something vital. Will your cook person be offended if I pick the bits out of this?'

'The bits?'

'The bits of lemon.' Kelly stuck a straw into the glass and chased the tiny pieces of lemon zest around. 'I'm not good with bitty things.'

Alekos inhaled deeply. 'I'll convey your preferences to my team.'

'*Team?* Gosh, how many people does it take to peel a couple of lemons?' She sipped her drink and sighed. 'Actually, it's delicious. Even with the bits. All right, this is all very nice—the whole private jet, pretty clothes and lemon-from-the-tree scene—but don't think I've forgiven you, Alekos. I still think you're a complete b—' her tongue tangled over the word '—bleep.'

'You think I'm a "bleep"? *What* is a "bleep"?'

'It's a substitute for a bad word that I absolutely don't want to say out loud.' Kelly snagged a few more bits of lemon with her straw. 'On television they stick a bleep sound in instead of the swear word. I'm doing the same thing.'

'Which swear word?'

'You have more intelligence than that, Alekos. Work it out for yourself.'

'You don't know one?'

'Of course I do.' Kelly sipped her drink slowly. 'But I'm always very careful with my language. I don't want to slip up in front of the children. I try never to swear, even when severely provoked.'

'I seem to recall that you called me a bastard.'

'Actually, you said that about yourself. I just agreed. It felt good, actually.' Kelly pressed the glass to her arms to cool her overheated skin. 'So why did you make me deliver the ring in person? Why not use a courier or send one of your staff? They can't all be peeling lemons.'

'I didn't want the ring. I wanted you.'

Kelly's heart tumbled and she put her glass down because her hands were suddenly shaking so much that they'd lost their ability to grip. 'You didn't want me four years ago.'

'Yes, I did.'

She looked up at him, reminding herself not to fall for anything he said. 'You have a funny way of showing it.'

'You are the first woman I have ever proposed to.'

'But not the last.'

'I did *not* propose to Marianna.'

'But you were going to.'

'I don't want to hear her name mentioned again. She has no relevance to our relationship. Tell me why you have black circles under your eyes.'

That's right, change the subject, Kelly thought moodily. He obviously didn't want to talk about Marianna. And maybe she didn't, either. 'I have black circles under my eyes because of you. Fighting you is exhausting.'

'Then don't fight me.'

Kelly wondered how her heart could still miss a beat even when her brain was issuing warning signals. Yes, he was gorgeous; there was no denying that he was gorgeous. Everything about him was designed to attract the opposite sex, from the leashed power in his broad shoulders to the haze of black hair revealed by his open-necked shirt. Desire pumped through her veins, her physical response contradicting her emotions.

Natural selection, she thought to herself, scrambling around for an excuse for the way she felt. It helped a little to pretend that she was genetically programmed to be attracted to the strongest, the fittest and the most powerful male of the species. And Alekos Zagorakis was all those things.

But just because she could feel herself sinking didn't mean she was prepared to go down without a fight.

Make a fool of herself as she had first time around? Throw herself at a man who didn't want her? No. Absolutely no. Not even knowing that she was carrying his child.

'If you expect me to just surrender to you then you'll be disappointed. I'll never be submissive.'

'I don't need submissive. I do want honest.'

'That's rich, coming from you. When did you ever tell me what you were truly feeling?'

A muscle flickered in his lean cheek, the merest hint of tension in a personality big on control. 'I don't find it easy to open up, that's true. I'm not like you. You spill out what you're feeling, when you're feeling it.'

'It's how I deal with things.'

'And I deal with things by myself. That's what I've always done. I have never felt the need to confide.'

Kelly picked up her drink again and sipped, brooding on the differences in their personalities. 'So I might as well go home, then.'

'No. There *are* things I need to tell you. Things I should have told you four years ago.'

Judging from his tone, they were going to be things she didn't want to hear. Kelly wondered uneasily if she should just tell him she was pregnant before he said something that would make her want to thump him. Being non-violent was becoming a real challenge around Alekos. 'Am I going to hate you for what you say?'

'I thought you already hated me.'

'I do. In which case, you might as well just get on with it and say whatever it is you want to say.' Ridiculously apprehensive, Kelly shrugged, trying to look cool and casual—as if whatever he said was going to make no difference to her. But it was obviously going to be something important, wasn't it? Whatever it was had stopped him from turning up on his wedding day, which was pretty major from anyone's point of view. And then there was the screaming tension she could feel pulsing from his powerful frame.

'Just say it, Alekos. I'm not great with all this suspense and tension stuff. I *hate* it on those TV shows where they say "and the winner is...", and then they wait ages and ages before they give you the answer, and you're thinking, "for goodness' sake, just get on with it".' Realising that he was looking at her as if she were demented, she gave a tiny shrug. 'What? What's wrong?'

Alekos shook his head slowly. 'You *never* say what I expect you to say.'

Kelly thumped her glass down on the table. 'I just want you to get to the point before the suspense kills me! I embarrassed you? I talked too much? I was messy?' She wrinkled her nose, trying to think which of her other sins might have been sufficient to send him running for the hills. 'I eat too much?'

'I love your body, I find your need to drop your belongings as you walk surprisingly endearing, I have always been fascinated by your ability to say exactly what is on your mind with no filter, and you have *never* embarrassed me.'

The angle of the sun had shifted and it reflected off his glossy dark hair. Somewhere close by an orange fell onto the ground with a dull thud, but Kelly didn't notice. She was too busy trying to hold back the sudden rush of hope that bounded free inside her, like a puppy suddenly let off a lead. 'I never embarrassed you? Not even once?'

'Not even once.' His hot, brooding gaze dropped to her mouth. 'But I seem to remember that I embarrassed you most of the time.'

Kelly turned scarlet. 'Only when we did it in broad daylight. Why do they call it that—why *broad* daylight? Why not narrow daylight?' Chattering nervously, she broke off as he ran his hand over his face and shook his head in exasperation.

'I'm trying to tell you something, and it isn't easy.'

'Well, please just get on with it! It's honestly not good for you to have this much stress. It furs up your arteries.' Her palms were sweating and her stomach was churning. It was like waiting for an exam result, she thought anxiously, her mind still jumping ahead. Perhaps it *was* the age thing that had caused him to walk away. Maybe he had been worried that she was too young to know her own mind. Or maybe he'd thought their relationship was too much of a whirlwind. If it had been the age thing, that was now fixed, wasn't it? She was older. The kids in her class thought she was positively ancient. She was probably less inhibited. Thinking of their steamy encounter on her kitchen table didn't do anything to alleviate the heat in her cheeks. *She was definitely less inhibited.*

All she had to do was assure him that she'd matured, that she knew her own mind. He'd apologise. She'd be hurt, but forgiving. Her mind sprinted ahead again, weaving happy endings from the threads of disaster.

Alekos breathed in deeply. 'The morning of the wedding I read an interview you'd given to a celebrity magazine. You'd spilled your guts about what you wanted. It was all there on the page.'

Still enjoying a fantasy about their future, Kelly tried to remember exactly what she'd said in that particular interview. 'The press were all over me. Apparently the fact that you'd never shown any interest in marrying anyone before suddenly made me interesting.'

He was going to be really pleased about the baby, she thought dreamily.

They'd live happily ever after. She'd ask him to buy a house in Little Molting; she could still teach her class in September, and once the baby was born they'd come back to Corfu and raise the child here, among the olive groves.

She smiled at Alekos, but he didn't smile back.

Instead his features were hard, like an exquisitely carved Greek statue. 'You said that all you'd ever wanted was a family. You said you wanted four children.'

'That's right.' Kelly wondered whether this would be a good moment to tell him that they already had one on the way. 'At least four.'

Muttering something in Greek, Alekos lifted his hand to the back of his neck, visibly struggling with what he had to say next. 'When I saw that article I realised that we had plunged into this relationship with no real thought to the future. It was all about the present. We hadn't discussed what either of us really wanted. I didn't know what you wanted until I read it in that magazine.' His voice was raw. 'It was only when I saw your interview that I realised we didn't want the same thing.'

'Oh?' Still bathing in her own little bubble-bath of happiness, Kelly gave an understanding smile. 'Honestly, I just wish you'd said something right away. I sort of forgot you were Greek. You always have big families, don't you? Four kids probably seems like nothing to you. We can have more. I'm not worried. I teach thirty back home! How many did you have in mind?'

Alekos closed his eyes briefly and pressed his fingers to the bridge of his nose. 'Kelly...'

'It doesn't worry me. I love kids. And I don't even expect you to do the nappies, as long as you help with all the other stuff.'

'Kelly.' He closed his hands over her shoulders, gripping tightly as he forced her to listen to him. 'I don't want a big family.' He waited a moment, apparently allowing time for those momentous words to penetrate her thin veneer of happiness. 'I don't want a family at all.'

Somehow, Kelly managed to make her mouth move. 'But—'

'I'm trying to tell you that I don't want children. I never did.'

CHAPTER FIVE

'*THEÉ MOU*, do something!' His tone dark and dangerous, Alekos glared at the local doctor. The guy had to be
almost seventy and appeared to have two speeds—slow
and stop. Fingering the phone in his pocket, Alekos
wondered how long it would take to fly a top physician
in from Athens. 'She banged her head really hard!'

'Was she knocked unconscious?'

Vibrating with impatience, Alekos thought back to
the hideous moment when Kelly's head had made contact with the glossy tiles. 'No, because she called me a
bleep several times.'

'A *bleep*?'

'Never mind. But she wasn't knocked out. I carried
her up to the bedroom and she's been lying here unconscious ever since.'

Glancing at him thoughtfully, the doctor touched the
bruise on Kelly's forehead. 'Why did she fall?'

Alekos felt the tension trickle down his spine. This
had to be the most uncomfortable conversation he'd
had in his life. 'She slipped on the tiles when she was
running.'

'And why was she running?'

Two hot spots of colour touched his cheeks and
guilt squeezed tight. 'Something had upset her.' Alekos

ground his teeth, wondering why he was explaining himself to a doctor so ancient he had undoubtedly known Hippocrates personally. '*I* upset her.'

Apparently unsurprised by that confession, the doctor reached into his bag and removed some pills. 'Nothing much changes there, then. I was called to see Kelly on the day of her wedding: the wedding that never happened.'

So, although he was slow, there was clearly nothing wrong with his memory. Alekos gritted his teeth. Everything that happened today appeared to be designed to make him feel bad. 'Kelly needed a doctor?'

'She was very shocked. And the press were savaging her.'

Feeling as though he'd been slugged in the stomach by a blunt instrument, Alekos drew his eyebrows together, shaken by that graphic description. 'She should have ignored them.'

'How? You're six-foot-three and intimidating,' the doctor said calmly. 'I don't think Kelly has ever been rude to anyone in her life. Even when she was struggling with what had happened, she was still polite to me. Leaving her to the mercy of the press was like throwing raw meat to sharks.'

Wincing at the analogy, Alekos felt as though he was being slowly boiled in oil. 'I may not have handled it as well as I could have done.'

'You didn't handle it at all. But that doesn't really surprise me. What surprised me was the fact that you'd asked her to marry you in the first place.' The doctor closed his case with a hand wrinkled with age and exposure to the sun. 'I remember you coming here to stay with your grandmother as a child. I remember one summer in particular, when you were six years old. You didn't speak for a month. You had suffered a terrible trauma.'

Feeling as though someone had tipped ice down his shirt, Alekos stepped back. 'Thank you for coming so promptly,' he said coldly and the doctor gave him a thoughtful look.

'Sometimes,' he said quietly, 'when a situation has affected someone greatly, it helps to examine the facts dispassionately and handle your fears in a rational manner.'

'Are you suggesting I'm irrational?'

'I think you were the unfortunate casualty of your parents' dysfunctional relationship.'

His emotions boiling, Alekos strode towards the bedroom door and yanked it open. 'Thank you for your advice,' he said smoothly, controlling himself with effort. 'However, what I really need to know is how long you expect Kelly to remain unconscious.'

'She isn't unconscious.' The doctor's tone was calm as he picked up his bag and walked towards the door. 'She's lying with her eyes shut. I suspect she just doesn't want to speak to you. Frankly, I don't blame her.'

'Open your eyes, Kelly.'

Ignoring his commanding tone, Kelly kept her eyes tightly shut.

She was going to lie here in this safe, dark place until she'd worked out what to do.

He didn't want children. It was just like her dad all over again, only worse.

How could she have been so completely and utterly stupid? How could she not have known?

'Just because you're not looking at me, doesn't mean I'm not here.' His voice rang with exasperation and something else: remorse? 'Look at me. We need to talk.'

What was there to talk about?

He didn't want kids and she was pregnant. As far as she could see, the conversation was over before it had even begun.

What was she going to do?

She was going to have to raise their child completely on her own.

Overwhelmed by the situation, Kelly screwed her eyes up tightly, wishing that she could magic herself back to her tiny cottage in Little Molting and lock the door on the world.

Through the haze of her panic she heard him say something in Greek. The next minute he'd rolled her onto her back and lowered his mouth to hers. Rigid with shock, Kelly lay there for a moment, and then the tip of his tongue traced the seam of her lips, his kiss so gentle that she gave a despairing whimper.

Sensation shot through her and she opened her eyes. 'Get off me, you miserable—' She thumped her fists against the solid muscle of his shoulders. 'I *hate* you, and I hate your horribly shiny floors. I hurt on the outside *and* the inside.'

Alekos grabbed her fists in his hands and pressed them back against the pillows. 'I thought you were non-violent.'

'That was before I met you.'

His answer to that was to lower his head again and deliver a slow, lingering kiss to the corner of her mouth. 'I'm sorry you fell. I'm sorry you hurt yourself.'

Kelly tried to turn her head away but his hand held her still. 'You hurt me far more than your floor. *Stop* doing that—stop kissing me. How dare you kiss me when this whole situation is so horribly complicated and impossible and—get *off* me!'

She tried to wriggle away from him but he shifted over her and used his weight to press her into the bed.

'For both our sakes, lie still,' he gritted. Kelly glared up at him but his hard, intense gaze filled her vision.

'You're not playing fair.' She needed to get away from him. She needed space to think about what was best for the baby.

'I play to win.'

'Well, I'm not in the game any more. I give up. I surrender.' Kelly twisted under him but he put one hand on her hip and held her still.

'*Stop* moving,' he breathed. 'Kelly, I know what I said upset you, but you wanted me to be honest. You said you wanted to know what I was thinking.'

'Well, how was I to know you were thinking such awful things?' She strained against him but that movement brought her into direct contact with his body so she stilled. 'You're Greek! You're supposed to want hundreds of children.'

His expression was suddenly guarded. 'I don't.'

'I gathered that.' Kelly gave a groan and squeezed her eyes shut. This scenario was so far removed from what she'd expected that she had no idea how to deal with it. She needed time to work things out. No matter what happened, this must *not* turn into one of those occasions where she just blurted out what was on her mind. No; this time she was going to think it through, come up with a strategic plan and implement it carefully. She'd tell him when the time was right—when she was properly prepared.

Once she'd made a decision, she'd share it with him, and not before.

Alekos traced gentle fingers over the bruise on her forehead. 'You ought to take the tablets the doctor left.'

Wincing with the pain, Kelly opened her eyes. 'I can't take them.'

'Why not?'

'Because I can't take tablets. Don't ask me why.'

'They will stop your head hurting.' Alekos sounded puzzled and a touch exasperated. 'You just swallow them. What's so hard about that?'

'I just don't want to take them.'

'Why?'

'I said, don't ask me why!'

'Just take them, Kelly.'

'*No*, because I don't want to take anything that might hurt the baby!' The words burst from her mouth like a dam breaking behind a force of water and she felt an immediate rush of anger directed towards herself and him. 'I didn't want to say that. I wasn't ready to tell you yet! I *told* you not to ask me why, but you pushed and pushed, didn't you? I'm going on an assertiveness course.'

Alekos looked as though he'd been shot through the head at close range. 'Baby?'

'I'm pregnant, OK? I'm expecting your baby,' Kelly shrieked. 'That's the baby you don't want, by the way. So I think you'll agree that we're in a bit of a fix.'

* * *

White-faced and shaking, Alekos slid into the driver's seat of the Ferrari, started the engine and pressed his foot to the floor.

Baby?

The word echoed through his brain along with all the associated feelings. A child depending on him. A child whose entire happiness was going to be his responsibility. *A child crying on his own.*

A thin film of sweat covered his brow; he swore fluently in Greek and pushed the car to its limits, taking the hairpin bends like a racing driver.

Only when a horn blared did he finally come to his senses.

Treading on the breaks, he stopped the car at the top of the hill, staring down across the olive groves towards the villa.

Kelly was down there somewhere, probably packing her bags.

Crying her heart out.

With a rough imprecation, Alekos looked away, trying to apply logic to a situation that required none.

A baby. All his life he'd avoided this exact situation.

And now.

Why had he been so careless?

But he knew the answer to that. One look at Kelly had driven rational thought from his head. Every time he went near her, he behaved in a way that was totally at odds with his ruthlessly structured life.

Yet it wouldn't have been possible to find a less suitable woman if he'd tried.

She wanted four children.

Alekos broke out into a sweat. *Just get your head round one*, he told himself. *That would be a start.*

One baby. One baby depending on him. One baby whose entire future happiness was in his hands.

Alekos lifted his fist to his forehead, his knuckles white. Until this moment he'd never known what it was like to be truly afraid. But right now, right at this moment, he knew fear.

Fear that he'd let the child down.

Fear that he'd let Kelly down.

If he got this wrong, if he blew this, a child would suffer. And he knew only too well how that felt.

'*Theé mou*, what are you doing on your feet? You should be lying down, resting.' His hoarse voice came from the doorway and Kelly quickly scrubbed away her tears, feeling a rush of pure relief that he was still in one piece.

He hadn't gone and done something stupid like driving off a cliff. He was still alive; she didn't have his death on her conscience. Now she could be angry without worrying.

She pulled her nose out of the suitcase she was packing and turned.

Alekos was standing in the doorway to the bedroom, looking like someone who had just dragged himself from the wreckage of a car accident.

Alarmed, she scanned him for signs of injury. Maybe he *had* driven his car off a cliff.

She was the one who had bumped her head, but he was obviously in a far worse state. The moment she'd delivered the news that she was pregnant, he'd sprang from the bed like a competitor in an Olympic sprint, and he'd been out of the starting gates before anyone had said 'go'.

But now he was back. And in a complete state, if his appearance was anything to go by.

His usually sleek hair was ruffled and his shirt was crumpled, but the resulting effect was one of such potent masculinity that the frantic crashing of her heart threatened to fracture her ribs.

If anything, Alekos was even more spectacularly attractive when he was feeling vulnerable than when he was strong and in control.

Kelly fought back an impulse to comfort him, reminding herself that this situation was already more than complicated.

This whole thing would have been easier if he hadn't come back.

She hated the way he made her feel. This was a man who had walked out on their wedding day. A man who had just told her he didn't want children.

So why did she just want to hug him?

'I wasn't expecting you back so soon. Normally it takes you four years to reappear after one of your avoidance sessions.' Not trusting herself not to cry again, Kelly turned her back on him and stuffed the final items of clothing into her suitcase. It didn't seem to matter what he said or what he did, he was still the most gorgeous man she'd ever seen, and just being in the same room as him was enough to send her pulse into overdrive. 'Jannis said you'd taken the Ferrari.' She snapped her mouth shut, remembering too late that she'd been determined not to let him know she'd been worried enough to check on him. Recalling the desperation in her tone when she'd asked Jannis if there were any steep cliffs close by, she blushed. 'What are you doing back here?'

'I live here.' He sounded impossibly Greek. He kicked the door shut with his foot and strode across the bedroom towards her. 'About the baby...'

'*My* baby, not *the* baby.' Her heart tumbled and Kelly tried to ram a shoe into her case. 'Why won't this stuff fit?'

'Because you haven't packed neatly.'

'Life is too short to fold stuff neatly!' Incredibly stressed, Kelly took her frustration out on the suitcase by ramming it shut. 'Life is too short for a lot of things, and being with you is one of them. I wish I'd never sold your stupid ring, I wish I'd never come to Corfu in my gap year and I wish I'd never walked across your stupid floor!"

Alekos looked at her in confusion. 'That was all in the wrong order.'

'I don't care if it was all the wrong order. Having your baby after we've split up is the wrong order, too! Everything in my life seems to happen in the wrong order. Most people think *then* act.' Planting her on the lid, she managed to snap the case shut. 'I act then think, and if that's not the wrong order I don't know what is.' Numb with misery, horrified with herself for losing it, Kelly flopped onto the edge of the bed, aware that Alekos was watching her with the same degree of caution he might show an unexploded bomb.

'You are *very* upset, and I can understand that, but you are forgetting that when I said those things to you I did *not* know you were pregnant.'

'What difference does that make?'

'I was not trying to hurt you.'

'That makes it worse. That shows you truly meant what you said, which puts us in a bit of a fix.' Kelly stood up and hauled the little case off the bed, closing her eyes as a sudden attack of dizziness assailed her. 'Get out of here, Alekos, before I kill you and hide your body under an olive tree.'

'You should not be lifting heavy weights.'

'Fine—I'll *drag* your body there. I won't lift it.'

'I meant the suitcase.' He breathed, and she pushed her hair out of her eyes, feeling foolish.

'Oh; right. I knew that. Obviously. But the suitcase is on wheels. I can push it all the way to Little Molting if I have to.' Grabbing the suitcase, she vowed never, ever to get involved with any man again—especially not a fiercely bright Greek man whose superior intellect made her feel the size of a grain of sand. Why hadn't it occurred to her that he didn't want children? Why hadn't she spotted that?

And what was she supposed to do now?

She was having a child he didn't want. She should have nothing more to do with him. His declaration should have killed her feelings stone dead.

She was still crazy about him. She loved him as much now as she had four years ago.

Wishing that love could be switched on and off as easily as her iPod, Kelly wondered what he was going to have to do to her before she fell out of love with him. Had she no self-respect?

Was this how her mother had felt when she'd realised that she was having the baby of a man who had no interest in being a father?

Alekos said something in Greek and jabbed his fingers through his hair. 'I blame myself for not even thinking that you might be *pregnant*.' His voice was hoarse